First Blush

A Meegs Miscellany

First Blush

A Meegs Miscellany

Robert Bruce Stewart

&

M.E. Meegs

Street Car Mysteries

Florence, Mass.

Street Car Mysteries

streetcarmysteries.com

To all the tireless wordsmiths

Contents

Introduction

It's a rare fictional character who can make the leap to author in her own right, but M.E. Meegs, aka Emmie Reese, has managed the task with her customary aplomb —as she herself will gladly tell you.

Whether solving crimes as Emmie, or settling scores as Meegs, she charms readers with her unwaveringly unique style, while confusing them with her astoundingly poor grasp of geography.

Her critics may take what shots they will. But no one can deny that when reading a work by this leading lady of letters, one knows one has left the world of the ordinary.

– Robert Bruce Stewart

The Birth of M.E. Meegs

by

Robert Bruce Stewart

I

It was in early February that we received news from Scotland Yard that Harry and I had solved the murder of Arden Coombs. Mr. Noakes, from the British Consulate, delivered the letter himself.

This was just six weeks after a Mr. Leverton, of the Pinkerton Detective Agency, visited the apartment, twice. Both times he spoke with my mother, who was visiting for Christmas. Of course I had no way of knowing there *was* a Mr. Leverton of the Pinkerton Detective Agency when I wrote of him, so it was all a little embarrassing and I was glad to have missed his calls.

That story had upset Harry more than I could have imagined. I knew he wasn't at all fond of the Pinks, but it wasn't until then that I realized the depth of his animosity. Naturally, I couldn't tell the story as exactly as it had transpired without compromising the privacy of our friends, the Ketchums. But Harry was right to point out that Leverton could just as easily have been an operative for Drummond's Detective Agency, or Newcome's, etc.

To placate him I set out to find a story that put the Pinks in a bad light. With the help of a man at the offices of the *Eagle*, I found just the thing. It had occurred in August, just before Harry had brought me to Brooklyn. Jacob Worth, a prominent political leader of the city, had had his watch stolen while attending the races at Brighton Beach. What made the story so absolutely priceless was that he was in the company of his close friend Robert Pinkerton, "the great detective." I wrote this up and showed it to Harry and he was overwhelmed by my gift. I suspect the new typewriter he presented me at Christmas was a sort of reward for furthering the cause that clearly meant so much to him, and not the acknowledgement of my development as a writer that he alleged. But if the periodic abusing of the Pinkertons is all it takes to content a husband, enough at least for him to overlook my small indiscretions, it seems a small price to pay.

I've strayed a bit from my explanation of Mr. Noakes's visit and shall go back to the beginning, the birth of M.E. Meegs. It began, at least in part, out of economic necessity. Harry and I were newly married and his business was slow. Harry is an insurance investigator, of sorts, and at that time was working by the job. But the interval between jobs could be long. And we had had a small setback, financially, while visiting recently in Glens Falls.

To be perfectly honest, I was partly responsible for the loss. But nearly every plunger at the track that day was likewise whipsawed by the infamous Searchlight. And I feel justified in pointing out that if you were to tot up my four days of gains against my one day of losses, you would see I am a net winner on the turf. Nonetheless, there is no arguing the fact that the loss in Glens Falls was untimely.

When we returned to Brooklyn, I resolved to take a hand in earning the family's bread. It had been my goal to become a writer since I was a freshman at college. Now I felt I had both the blessing of time and the incentive of looming poverty. Harry had mentioned a friend who made a living as a writer of dime novels so I thought I would pay the gentleman a visit and ask his advice. I wrote this Mr. Ulmer with just the town as an address and received a very friendly invitation in reply.

Harry was to be away for a week, so I decided this was the time to strike. I left the apartment just after Harry and used the money he had given me to put toward the grocer's account to buy a ticket on the Long Island Railroad. It was a rather long train ride out to Good Ground and when I disembarked there was no one else about. The directions Mr. Ulmer had sent didn't correspond particularly well with the configuration of streets before me, so I stopped in a small grocer's. The proprietor said he knew exactly where the Ulmers' cottage was and provided me with directions that bore no resemblance at all to Mr. Ulmer's. After an hour of trudging about various country lanes, I found the Ulmers' cottage.

I was greeted by the Ulmers' eleven-year-old daughter, a girl of remarkable poise. Mrs. Ulmer was busily typing a manuscript that needed to make the evening mail and after welcoming me, in a very friendly manner, she returned to work. There were two other children and Mr. Ulmer, who was writing the manuscript just as his wife was typing it. The youngest child, who could have been no more than five or six, had the task of relaying the handwritten pages from his father to his eldest sister, who would quickly scan them for errors, and from her to his mother. The middle child, a little girl of seven or eight, lay on the floor with a large dictionary and would look up words when called upon by her parents or sister.

I had a very pleasant conversation with Mr. and Mrs. Ulmer, during which time neither of them paused from their work for more than a moment. Mr. Ulmer informed me that while the demand for dime novels and the nickel weeklies was quite steady, he wasn't sure he would recommend the field to a newcomer, as the meager pay per page necessitated the hectic conditions I was witnessing. He told me he had received a letter from a British agent in New York who was looking for news stories of a sensational nature to be sent back to Britain for publication.

"Perhaps you would find that work rewarding?" he offered.

"I've never written for a newspaper," I confessed. "Only short fictional pieces."

"Oh, that doesn't matter," he assured me. "They'd be going to England, or Wales.... The readers there would never know if they were true or not. All that matters is that they be sensational. And short. You know the thing: 'by telegraph from our New York correspondent.'"

"You mean I could just sort of make things up?" I asked.

"Why not?" Mrs. Ulmer pointed out. "That's what the papers here do."

She had a lovely laugh, and the whole household seemed quite happy in its work. Mr. Ulmer found me the agent's card and offered to sell me his old typewriter for four dollars. It was an ancient thing, but it did seem to work, as long as you typed slowly. Much more slowly than Mrs. Ulmer's pace. I paid him out of the money Harry had given me to pay the butcher.

Then Mrs. Ulmer asked Celeste, the eldest girl, to walk me to the station so I wouldn't become lost. It was only after both her parents assured her that they would be extra vigilant during her absence that she agreed to do so.

I asked Celeste if she enjoyed working with her parents and if she didn't miss playing with other children. It was, after all, a sort of literary sweatshop, though I didn't use that term. She said the frantic pace I had witnessed lasted only three or four days. Then the family spent several days together picnicking at the beach, reading, and putting on shows for each other.

I inquired about which books she most enjoyed and I mentioned titles I had read as a girl. She wasn't familiar with any of them. But she had read all of Austen and the Brontës and most of Dickens and George Eliot, and proceeded to mention a dozen others—three of whom were unknown to me. When she asked me which novels I had read, I tried, with increasing desperation, to come up with titles with which she was unfamiliar. I was on the point of inventing an author when she came to my rescue. She said that if I had been to college, as I had mentioned, I must have read in Latin. I lied shamelessly and told her that nothing had thrilled me so as Caesar's discourse on the three parts of Gaul.

When we reached a point where the station was in view, she said good-bye and returned to her editorial duties at full charge. We had shared the burden of the typewriter until then, and I found it quite unwieldy carrying it on my own. By the time I reached the station, I was fairly exhausted. When I disembarked at the Flatbush Avenue station, I realized there was no way I could negotiate my way on the street car with my load. I couldn't bear the thought of walking the ten blocks to the apartment, so instead hired a cab with the last fifty cents of the butcher's money.

The next day, I visited the Manhattan office of Baily & Sackett. It was only Mr. Sackett, really, in a small office he rented from a larger firm. He greeted me enthusiastically and like Mr. Ulmer assured me my lack of experience would not be an encumbrance. He explained that he would receive my stories and then try to place them in various publications throughout Great Britain. The only one he mentioned specifically was the *Pall Mall Gazette*. I would be paid for each placement, after he had deducted a small fee for his services. He said I could write about whatever I wished, but to keep in mind that the more sensational the better. As an example, he said a fire in a tenement was all well and good, but a fire in a tenement where a brave fireman climbs through flames to reach a baby mislaid by her mother, and then escapes by balancing the child on his head as he jumps from roof to roof would be much more the thing. He suggested I should aim for between two hundred and fifty and five hundred words, as anything longer would be much harder to place.

I was very excited and rushed back to Brooklyn to begin a story I had already conceived. But first, I needed to purchase a new ribbon for the typewriter, and then spent most of the rest of the day cleaning the well-worn keys. Much of the next morning was given up to the creation of an appropriate pen name. I finally settled on M.E. Meegs. "M.E." for the phonetic connection to Emmie, and Meegs simply because it sounded like the name of a Fleet Street hack.

This brings me to the story that prompted the visit from Mr. Noakes, of the British Consulate. But before I begin, I need to explain a little about what happened in Buffalo. Put simply, my uncle had been leading a double life, faked his death, twice, and then was gunned down in Toronto. Harry and I solved that case, back in early August, and in a way, I suppose, it led to our marriage. But my original explanation for my uncle's disappearance was that he had been killed by confederates in a ring of opium smugglers. And that they had then staged a yachting accident while keeping his body submerged in the Erie Canal. When the body had deteriorated enough that the cause of death could no longer be determined, they would make it appear as if it had washed up on the lake shore, several months after the supposed accident.

I must admit, I was genuinely disappointed when it turned out otherwise. But now I was free to write an account of the crime as it *should* have transpired. In fact, my version was much more befitting of Mr. Sackett's requirements than the too-prosaic truth.

It took no time to write a story of the appropriate length, and I brought it to Mr. Sackett the first thing Monday morning, August 27th. He was very pleased with it and thought he would have no trouble placing it. I asked what that would pay and he said one and six, in British currency of course. I wasn't entirely sure what that translated to in dollars, and yet I didn't want to appear ignorant by asking. So, on the way home, I stopped at the library and learned that one British pound was equal to almost five dollars, and six shillings was another dollar and fifty cents.

II

In the meantime, I had learned that the horses were running at Sheepshead Bay. So, that afternoon, I took the money meant for the laundry and went out to the track in the hopes of winning enough to pay the grocer and butcher. Sheepshead Bay was a huge affair, unlike any race course I had seen before, and I found it not a little intimidating. In my previous visits to race courses, gentlemen I was with had placed my bets for me. I was most confused by the posted notices on the exterior walls of the building I had been told was the betting pavilion. These signs stated emphatically that "pool-selling, bookmaking, or any other kind of gambling" was prohibited. A friendly gentleman assured me this was simply a clever joke on the part of the State of New York, though the humor of it escaped me.

Once inside, I wandered about the pavilion, where there were a number of bookmakers taking bets. They sat on high stools and periodically held up long, narrow slates with the odds they were offering on the horses entered in the next race. Below them, their clerks recorded the bets. As each race was called, there was a mad rush out to the track, then the bookmakers quickly returned, followed by their eager customers. I found the stampedes so disquieting that I stayed to the far side of the pavilion and never saw the actual races. It was through nothing but sheer luck that I managed to parlay my four dollars into six.

There was still one race to run, but I decided I had

done as well as I could hope to playing the game blindly. As I neared the exit I was accosted by a man in a large bowler hat.

"No unescorted ladies, Miss." He said this in a very officious manner, and he gave me quite a start. But then he smiled and added, "Sorry, Miss. I was only having fun."

Then he introduced himself. His name was Mr. Larabee. I gave my own name as Miss Meegs. He told me he had seen me studying the bookmakers' stalls and wondered what sort of technique I was using. I confessed to him I was a novice, and had won what little I had through luck and luck alone. He suggested that depending on luck at a race track was not at all prudent. He gave me a brief explanation of what was going on and the arcane legal reasons for the methodology.

All through this conversation, he was distracted by the gestures of several tall men about the pavilion. Every once in a while, he would gesture back. As politely as possible, I asked if he would confide in me what he and his associates were communicating. And he very affably did so.

He and his fellows were trying to find discrepancies in the odds offered by the various bookies. In general, he told me, the odds are against the bettor and the bookmakers knew how to manage their pools. But sometimes a bookmaker eliminates certain horses from his pool by refusing to take bets on those he thinks likely to win. Assuming the bookmaker consistently picked the winners, this was a very lucrative proposition. Success with it inevitably led the bookmaker to offer longer odds on the horses he was taking bets on to attract more customers. And when he did, Mr. Larabee and his confederates pounced. In essence, the bookmaker became the gambler and Larabee & Co. the house.

"The profit isn't large, Miss Meegs. But it's a living." He returned some signals and then added, "There might be a job in it for you if you're interested."

"What sort of job?" I asked.

"Well, me and the men you see are all known. The bookies won't take our bets. When I signal one of those gents, he gives a little sign to someone else, who makes the bet."

"I'm afraid I'm not interested in a position of this kind," I said. But not wanting to give offense, I added, "Though it is wonderfully inventive."

"Thank you, Miss Meegs. But you see, it wouldn't be a regular position. You could do it whenever it was convenient, like today." Then he very obviously looked at my left hand. "Is your husband away, Miss?"

There was no point in making a denial, so I told him my husband was away, and that my name wasn't Meegs. He said that was fine, because his name wasn't Larabee. In fact, he wasn't sure he knew the real names of any of his associates. Harry wouldn't return until late the next evening, so I agreed to meet Mr. Larabee that afternoon so he could brief me on the procedure. He gave me the address of a cottage off of Ocean Avenue, just beyond the track, and told me from now on to only speak to him there.

There was nothing to it, really, for my part. I was given three hundred dollars to make wagers with and taught a few simple signs. The key thing was to keep in a position where I could see the man giving me the signs, one of the tall men, without it being apparent to the bookie I was doing so. I had some doubts as to the legality of Mr. Larabee's business, so I was relieved that a policeman was in the cottage eating a hearty lunch. He had to have overheard the entire conversation, yet he never looked up from his newspaper and seemed completely indifferent.

We—myself and my tall accomplice—were positioned near a bookmaker who had just seven horses on his slate, while there were at least ten running in the first race. For the first two races, I received no signs. I made small bets on my own account, but lost both times. In the third race, I received the first sign. I was to bet an equal amount on all the odd number horses. I had been instructed to always bet the entire amount, so I did so. Seventy-five dollars on each horse. We lost. I still had a couple dollars of my own, so I thought I'd stay for one more race. Then a small boy selling news sheets came up beside me and slipped me an envelope. It contained six hundred dollars. There was no sign in the fourth race, and I lost the last of my own small bank. Then, just before the fifth race, I had a sign and bet the six hundred as instructed. We lost again.

I returned to the cottage and found Mr. Larabee handing out envelopes to his associates, and sometimes receiving them in return. Some of these people were the tall men, but some looked like prosperous businessmen. I felt a little sheepish approaching him, not having any envelope to give him. But he said that I shouldn't worry about that, as they had actually done quite well that day. He handed me an envelope which contained twenty-five dollars. On the way home, I stopped off and paid the butcher, the grocer, and the laundry, and still had eight dollars.

That evening I told Harry about my endeavor and he

seemed sincerely pleased. I mean, of course, my literary endeavor. Though I hadn't received payment yet, I insisted we go out and celebrate, and the following Friday we went out to Manhattan Beach. That was the Friday before Labor Day. We had dinner at the hotel, then saw a show at the little theatre, and afterwards attended the fireworks.

I told Harry I was using some money my Aunt Nell had sent, but in fact it was the last of the money Mr. Larabee had paid me. In a way, I was glad things had worked out as they had, because when Harry made me swear I hadn't won it at the track, there was no need to deceive him.

Then I had a bit of a blow. On the way home Harry asked me how much I was being paid. I told him the one and six figure and that that would equal a little more than six dollars.

"Did Mr. Sackett say 'one and six' and just that?" he asked.

"Yes, that's the way they always express it," I said.

"Well, Emmie, I'm no authority on matters of international finance, but I believe when an Englishman says one and six, he means one shilling and six pence."

"What about the pounds?" I asked.

"What about the pounds, indeed?"

"Are you playing horse with me, Harry?" He had a habit of teasing me in a most disagreeable way. He just smiled. Well, he turned out to be correct in this instance. Harry also had a habit of being correct in a most disagreeable way.

As luck would have it, a check for three hundred dollars arrived the next week. This was payment from an insurance company for our work in Buffalo, which had allowed it to forgo payment on a claim. It came to Harry, but honestly, it was more mine than his. I had arranged the contract and, in the end, it was my solution to my uncle's murder that allowed the company to withhold payment. And Harry conceded as much.

Now we felt ourselves supremely well-off. So much so, we actually made current one of the department store accounts. Harry took me to several Broadway shows, each after a dinner at Delmonico's or Sherry's. And the fact I was only getting thirty-odd cents for each placement no longer seemed important.

It was then that I wrote the account of Mr. Leverton and his fierce fight against the white slavers of Sag Harbor. The battle culminated in a victory for Leverton and, the next morning, his rescue of 147 immigrant girls from a cave above the shore. One fair maiden, an orphan, of course, had caught Leverton's eye. Though I left it somewhat ambiguous as to whether she was in fact still a maiden at the time of said rescue, Mr. Leverton seemed content to leave the matter unexplored and married the girl. This was a sort of paraphrasing of what had occurred in Glens Falls just a month earlier.

Mr. Sackett told me this story was even better than the last. Then he said he had some very good news. He had placed my body-in-the-canal story and gave me my first payment: thirty-seven cents. He had quite generously rounded up the fraction of a cent.

"Where will the story run?" I asked. "Was it the *Pall Mall Gazette*?"

"No, not this go-round," he smiled. "It already ran, in the *Bacup Times*."

"I don't believe I've heard of the *Bacup Times*, or of Bacup, for that matter."

"Well," he said, "it's a modest placement, there's no denying that. But there are advantages to a modest placement. You see, now I can continue placing the same story elsewhere. Whereas, if it had made it into the *Pall Mall Gazette*, the whole of England would have seen it already."

I suppose his reasoning was sound. Still, I felt a little silly telling Harry my first placement was in the *Bacup Times*. He asked me if this was a sister publication of the *Hiccup Herald*. Harry hadn't had a chance to read either story, so now I told him all about them. He was very amused at the body-in-the-canal story and said it was destined to be a classic.

However, the second story, having a Pink as hero, he took as a slap in the face. As I mentioned earlier, Harry despised the Pinks and considered anyone who didn't share his view something of a traitor. A week or so later, I came up with the antidote story, about Mr. Worth, Robert Pinkerton's friend, having his pocket picked in Pinkerton's presence. Harry loved this story, and I was back in his good graces.

We went through our three hundred dollars at a staggering pace. In three weeks there was nothing left and we were back on account at the grocer, butcher, and laundry. In Buffalo, my annual salary hadn't been much more than that check. Harry's work was still slow, so he felt he had no choice but to go back on the payroll at his former employer. He made an awful show of despair. Harry had a sort of religious prohibition against working normal business hours. As for my contribution to the family purse, Mr. Sackett paid almost enough to cover the fare I spent collecting my fee. And the season at the track was now over. It seemed obvious I would need to find a more remunerative way of augmenting our income.

It was then that I first heard about Mrs. Holden's little card parties. I was having coffee with Dorothy, our maid. Harry had hired Dorothy to come in three times a week, before we were married. And when he returned with me, neither of us had the heart to let her go. If I hinted that maybe someone else could better take advantage of her services, she went into a litany of sad tales about her family. The tales were so detailed that some of them may have actually been true, so I made note of them all.

Well, on the day in question, I had brought home some pastries and was sharing them with Dorothy over coffee. I enjoyed chatting with her because she was acquainted with a side of Brooklyn of which Harry seemed unaware, the Brooklyn of policy shops and Raines Law hotels. She told me about her family's adventures, and those of her friends, most of whom also worked as domestics. This led her to Nancy, a live-in girl employed by Mrs. Holden, just up the street at the Margaret.

It seems that on two afternoons a week, while her husband was away at work, Mrs. Holden held card parties for her friends. But these ladies weren't playing whist for five cents a hand, they were playing bridge for ten cents a point.

I had been developing a certain skill with cards ever since meeting an associate of Harry's named Mr. Schuler, back in Buffalo. I had every confidence I could come out ahead if I could just get invited to Mrs. Holden's card parties. Dorothy suggested that if we made Nancy a confederate, she could find some suitably subtle way of letting Mrs. Holden know there was another willing attendee nearby. I gave her a few dollars to take Nancy out on her next evening off and that was all it took. A day later, I received an invitation from Mrs. Holden.

Which brings me to the first visit of Mr. Noakes. This was sometime in the latter half of October. He was a young man, with sandy hair and a hurried way of speaking that sometimes made it difficult to understand what exactly he was saying. That and his accent, of course. Mr. Sackett had given him my address and he said he was much relieved to find me at home.

"You see—Mrs. Meegs, is it?" he asked.

"Mrs. Reese," I told him. "M.E. Meegs is just a pen name."

"Oh, yes, of course. Well, you see, Mrs. Reese, about a month ago, a body was found in the Rochdale Canal, in Lancashire."

"Are you friend of Harry's?" I was certain this must be an elaborate scheme of Harry's to have me look like a fool. He was convinced that I had a predilection for bodies in canals.

"I'm afraid I don't know Harry, Mrs. Reese. Is he an associate of Mr. Sackett?"

"I'm sorry, Mr. Noakes, please go on."

"Well, let's see, where was I? Oh, yes, this body was found when the police were coincidentally dredging that part of the canal for a missing girl, who, as it turned out, had eloped with a circus performer. This man, not the circus performer, the dead man in the canal, Arden Coombs was his name, was found with the pockets of his coat filled with stones. So, at first, the police assumed he had committed suicide by drowning himself in the canal."

"At first?"

"Yes, you see, there was a large contusion on the side of Mr. Coombs's head, and the doctor said it was most unlikely it had been caused by a fall. He also said Mr. Coombs had been dead no more than a day or two. In one pocket of the coat there was a newspaper clipping. It was barely legible but the police eventually determined it was a clipping from the *Bacup Times*. The editor told the police the story had come from a source here, in New York. It was your story, Mrs. Reese.

"Well, the Lancashire Constabulary thought it highly suggestive that a man found dead in a canal carried with him an article about a man found dead in a canal. Especially now that it was determined that he'd been murdered. It was the only clue of any sort they had, so they contacted the Consul here for help. He assigned me to find out what I could. I contacted the authorities in Buffalo and soon determined that no such incident had occurred there, at least not in anyone's memory. Bodies had been found in the Erie Canal, I was told, but none of the details matched the case in the clipping. I then learned the story came from Mr. Sackett. At first, he was reluctant to give me your address, but the Consul made a call to the police commissioner, and, well, here I am."

"I see," I said. I hardly need to point out that the situation was an awkward one. I wasn't sure how to approach the matter, but I decided to simply tell my tale and hope for the best. "Mr. Noakes, I'm sure you're aware that newspapers sometimes take certain liberties with the facts in cases like this."

"Certainly, Mrs. Reese. You see, my father's in the business. But in this case, which are the true facts?"

"Well, there was a ring of opium smugglers, or at

least there probably was such a ring. And a man was killed and his body thrown into a canal, or slip, more precisely. And he was very likely to have been involved in the smuggling ring, assuming it existed, of course. Though he was murdered for another reason entirely. And all that had nothing really to do with the other man, the one who never had a yachting accident."

"I see. And the names?"

"All taken from the previous evening's *Brooklyn Daily Eagle*."

"I see. Well, I suppose it could just be a coincidence."

"That seems very unlikely, Mr. Noakes. Are there any suspects?"

"Well, I was only given a summary of the situation, but from what I gather, no, there aren't. Apparently, Mr. Coombs was a well-respected, and well-liked, solicitor. He was an older gentleman and had already turned his practice over to his son, with whom he lived. There is no one who seems to have a motive."

"Have they determined whose coat Mr. Coombs was wearing?"

"Whose coat, Mrs. Reese?"

"Well, it hardly seems likely Mr. Coombs clipped my story. Unless he anticipated being murdered in this way."

"I see what you mean. I'm not sure if the police there have thought of that or not. I shall have to cable them your question, Mrs. Reese."

He assured me he would let me know if he learned anything new and then said good-bye. I decided not to tell Harry about Mr. Noakes's visit. If I did, he would go on, in his jocular sort of way, about how I had been the cause of poor Mr. Coombs's death.

That same day, I got word from Mr. Sackett that he had placed the story about Leverton and the white slavers in the *Leek Times and Cheadle News*. Of course I didn't relay this to Harry, partly because I didn't want to suffer his wrath, and partly because I would have felt distinctly silly repeating the name of the publication.

III

For my next story, I used as a basis an episode that had received much attention in New York. A lawyer named Henry Zeimer had been operating what was termed a divorce mill. If a wife became tired of her husband, something not altogether unimaginable, she could hire Mr. Zeimer and he would provide a young lady to act as co-respondent in a divorce suit. They would subpoena this woman and she would, reluctantly, confess to having had relations with said husband. The husband could, of course, make denials, but then they always do. If the husband were suing for divorce, the same young lady might appear as a private detective, giving evidence against the wife. I told the story in the voice of this young lady. I had met many consummate actresses of this type at college and had much fun coming up with the details left out of the newspaper accounts. It turned out a little longer than Mr. Sackett would have liked, but he said he was sure he could place it somewhere.

Mrs. Holden's card parties had proved moderately profitable, at least until she confided that some of the other ladies were having suspicions about my "fancy work" with the cards. I took her caution to heart and after that my winnings became more modest. The attendees were mainly middle-aged, middle-class women who held conventional views on just about everything. I was generally able to get along with them, but apparently committed a faux pas when I asked if Mrs. Holden minded living across from the huge stables that occupied the opposite corner. She replied, rather emphatically, that this was the Brooklyn Riding and Driving Club, and not some common livery. I offered a contrite apology, but of course they smell just the same.

My next story again came from the *Eagle*. A man claimed that he had been robbed of $1,800 by two women with whom he was having a conversation on Patchen Avenue, at three o'clock in the morning. This man was "well known among the fraternity of the Turf" and often carried such sums. What made this case so singular was that the money had been taken from a wallet in his trousers, and then the wallet returned, without him being aware until the next day. At least one of these women was a master gun, or dip, if you prefer that term. I credited her with a veritable crime wave.

Mr. Worth, the friend of Robert Pinkerton, was also robbed by an unknown young woman. At least he was in my version of the event. I decided it would be more interesting if I made it the *same* woman. I chose an exotic name I'd seen on a shop window and paid tribute to her talents with an aristocratic title. And so it was that the Countess Consuelo Maria de la Salsiccia was christened, the scion of a noble Italian family.

Then, just around the first of December, Mr. Noakes telephoned and asked if he could drop by that evening. He had received a letter from an Inspector Cropsey of the Lancashire Constabulary and wanted to share it with me. Over dinner, I told Harry all about Mr. Noakes's previous visit. Ironically, he thought I was having fun with him. It wasn't until Mr. Noakes came to the door that he seemed to comprehend the truth of it.

I introduced the two of them and then Mr. Noakes sat down and read us aloud the letter, which follows.

Dear Noakes,

Please inform Mrs. Reese that she was correct about the coat. Mr. Coombs's son had identified it as his father's, and it was very similar. But after your inquiry, I looked into it further and it seems the elder Mr. Coombs's coat was by a different maker. Mrs. Coombs, Arden's daughter-in-law, insists the label is not the same. Old Coombs's coat, however, cannot be found.

Now it seems even more likely that this is a case of murder. Unfortunately, I can find neither a suspect or a motive. Mr. Coombs was a widower of sixty-two years, exceptionally well liked by colleagues, family, and friends. The only mark anyone had against him was his poor choice of attire, hardly a motive for murder.

The two usual motives, money and love, seem both eliminated. His estate consisted mainly of his well-established practice as a solicitor, which he had already turned over to his son. Beyond a few hundred pounds in the bank, his son isn't aware of any other asset. There was a modest insurance policy, but his son spent more than that on the monument over his grave.

As it happens, the deceased had been having a fling of sorts with a woman, but she is likewise widowed and I can find no one who held any objection to the affair.

No evidence has been recovered at the canal, where the body was found. It had rained quite a lot the evening before it was discovered and there were no clear tracks apparent. It is a somewhat secluded stretch and there seems to have been no witness, though I still have to locate a canalman and his family who passed through that previous afternoon.

For the lack of anything to the contrary, we are

working on the assumption this was the work of a stranger, someone simply passing by, perhaps a robbery gone awry. However, that does beg the question of Mrs. Reese's story being in the pocket of the coat.

Please thank Mrs. Reese for her helpful suggestion. I will inform you if there are any further developments, as I imagine she will be curious to find out what role her story played.

Regards,
Inspector Reginald Cropsey, Lancs. Constabulary

Mr. Noakes left us soon afterward and Harry and I spent the rest of the evening, and many subsequent evenings, pondering the strange circumstances of Arden Coombs's death.

It was about this time I had my big haul at Mrs. Holden's. I was particularly proud of it because it was achieved almost exclusively by bluff. I won over two hundred dollars that day, but of course could say nothing to Harry about it.

That same evening, Harry flew into the apartment like an excited child and shouted, "Tontine!"

"Are we speaking a foreign tongue this evening?" I asked.

"Emmie, don't you know what a tontine is? And you a college girl."

"All right, Harry. What is a tontine?"

"A tontine is a kind of primitive insurance fund, combined with a sort of lottery. And while it has many flaws as a financial scheme, as a literary device..."

"What is it, precisely?"

"Well, it can take many forms. But in our case, suppose a man like Arden Coombs wants to provide for his years of dotage, or perhaps he has a wife he cares for and wants to see that she has a comfortable widowhood. But what holds him back is that he might die before his dotage. He will have saved for nothing, especially if his widow was of the quarrelsome variety." He smiled, but I was impassive. "Well, what if he teams up with, say, two dozen of his fellows. All of about the same age, say forty. They all agree to put money into this fund, invest it, and then, in a set amount of time, say twenty years, distribute it to those who survive, with maybe third shares going to widows."

"Third shares?"

"Emmie, I'm not responsible for the attitudes of hypothetical Englishmen towards their wives. Now, the actuarial tables would tell you that 37.4% of these men will die in the intervening twenty years."

"37.4%?"

"Yes, give or take a tenth of a percent. So the 62.6% who survive will receive a sum at least 50% larger than they would have if they had depended on their own savings."

"Assuming no widows are allowed to survive."

"Apparently, they were all invalids and died tragically young."

"So you are suggesting that perhaps Mr. Coombs was a member of such a tontine and the other members conspired to kill him so they would receive a slightly larger share?"

"I spent most of the afternoon on this, Emmie, and I have a scenario Mr. Stevenson himself would have to admire. Say there were only nine or ten men in the tontine. And say the men making the investments had chosen particularly well. Then, through pure chance, they suffer an unusually high mortality rate. So there are only two or three left as the date for the distribution approaches."

"So now each death would mean a much greater share for the survivors."

"Yes, exactly."

"But why wouldn't Mr. Coombs's son know about the tontine?"

"Well, say our culprit, Mr. Highbottom, was the one charged with monitoring the investments of the tontine's trustees. Perhaps, years ago, he led Mr. Coombs to believe that most of it had been lost in one panic or another. Mr. Coombs, being a fairly prosperous and good-natured fellow, simply put the tontine out of his mind."

"Why cry over spilt milk? I see." In fact, I had to go over it in my head once more before I did see. "Yes, that is a marvelous plot, Harry."

"I thought you'd like it. You can consider it your Christmas present, Emmie."

"I was hoping for something a little more tangible."

"There's always hope, Emmie, when all else is lost."

I telephoned Mr. Noakes and suggested he ask Inspector Cropsey about the possibility of a tontine. He said he would and would let me know what response he received.

Harry's teasing me about my Christmas present had given me an idea. Harry had inherited a watch fob from a great uncle of his. In the locket, Harry had found a ticket from a Manhattan pawnbroker, which he assumed to be for the watch itself. A few years later, when he moved to New York, Harry looked up the pawnbroker, but the watch had been auctioned long before.

Harry loved to wear his watchless fob. If someone asked him the time, he would pull out the fob and say, "Good Lord, I've been robbed!" Although sometimes, he would take the ticket out of the locket and tell a tale about having to sell the watch to pay for the fob.

We'd only been married a few months and I'd grown weary of both versions. So I used part of my winnings from Mrs. Holden's to buy him a very respectable antique watch. Then I had a truly wonderful inspiration. I had an inscription made, which read:

Signor Reese,

I am returning your uncle's watch, as the Count says Mr. Worth's keeps much better time.

The Countess de la Salsiccia

The week before Christmas my mother arrived. She didn't think much of Dorothy's and my efforts at keeping house and spent much of her visit cleaning. One morning, while I was out shopping and she was disassembling the stove, Mr. Leverton stopped by and asked for M.E. Meegs. She told him there was no one by the name of Meegs residing here, and he apologized. When mother told me about it, of course I assumed it was some friend of Harry's. But he came a second time a few days later, and this time left a card. I was at Mrs. Holden's, and he interrupted mother giving Dorothy instructions on cleaning the crevices between the floor boards. I was relieved, because I had decided not to contact Mr. Leverton. If he was displeased with my story, the interview would be unpleasant. If he was pleased with it, he was liable to give me some attention that would upset Harry. I don't mean out of jealousy, but because of his antipathy for all things Pinkerton.

We had promised to take mother to the Christmas High Mass at Saint Patrick's Cathedral—only later learning it began at four-thirty in the morning. It was truly impressive, and even Harry pronounced it quite a show. After the mass we returned home and had a large breakfast. Harry gave me my new typewriter and a copy of *The Wrong Box*. I presented him with the edition of *Vanity Fair* which commemorated Mrs. Fiske's production of the play based on the book *Becky Sharp*. We gave mother a very colorful print of St. Patrick's.

Then Harry went down for a nap and I was able to take the opportunity to attach the watch to his fob without waking him. Later, I prompted mother to ask Harry the time. My memory of Harry's expression when he found the watch on his fob is one I will always treasure.

"Oh," I said, "has it turned up?"

"Yes," he smiled, "apparently some kind soul has redeemed my heirloom."

"Do check the inscription, Harry, to make sure there's been no mistake."

Though Harry enjoyed my joke immensely, I hadn't solved the problem as I had intended. Harry now loved to pull his watch out, show the inscription, and tell the long tale behind it, beginning with his uncle's demise and ending with the story of Mr. Worth's robbery in the presence of the despised Pinkerton. All I had achieved was to turn his wearisome joke into a tedious anecdote.

IV

A few days later, we returned to the apartment from putting mother on the train to find Mr. Noakes waiting for us. He had had another letter from Inspector Cropsey. He read it aloud:

Dear Noakes,

You may tell Mrs. Reese that she was correct. There was a tontine. Michael Coombs, Arden Coombs's son, found a record of it while going through his father's papers. But since his father's death rendered the family's position moot, he thought it of no consequence. Yet it does seem likely the murder of Arden Coombs is tied to this tontine in some way, even if how remains for now a mystery.

Thirteen men entered into the tontine in 1876. The accumulated investments of the group would be distributed to the surviving members in twenty-five years. However, if at any time all but one of the subscribers had passed on, the lone survivor would receive the funds immediately.

By last March, there were three survivors. Then Mr. Seymour Whitley, one of the three, died of heart failure. There was nothing suspicious about his death, but we are looking again at all the evidence. This left only Mr. Coombs and a Mr. Joseph Brayton.

I found that Brayton had visited the area of Rochdale not long before Mr. Coombs's murder, though he had an alibi for the time of the murder itself. To my mind, this indicated that Brayton had entered into a conspiracy with someone close to Mr. Coombs. And, indeed, that proved to be the case.

I confronted Mr. Brayton and told him it would likely end with him charged with murder. This was enough to compel him to tell his fantastic tale. It was, he says, Mr. Arden Coombs whom he had visited, at the latter's summons. Coombs proposed that they draw lots, with the loser agreeing to disappear. And to do so in a way that would lead the authorities to presume this man was dead. Falling overboard on a cruise was mentioned as a possibility. Then, when the apparent sole survivor collected the tontine's fortune, he would divide it equally with the other, who would be living somewhere in seclusion.

Brayton insists he saw Coombs's proposition as a symptom of senility, but went along with the game to humor him. Coombs lost, and agreed to undertake the subterfuge. Brayton insists nothing was said about the details of the plan, only that Coombs would find a means of contacting Brayton after he had received the payment.

When Brayton heard of Coombs's death, he suspected that he had succeeded in his ruse. But the thought that Coombs had killed another man in order to use his corpse troubled him. He went to Coombs's funeral and in paying his respects discovered that the dead man was in fact Arden Coombs. This is all on the word of Brayton, and he could offer no evidence, beyond his own testimony, that it had taken place as he described.

It was a far-fetched story, but I thought I would see if any arrangements had been made by Arden Coombs that might indicate there was some truth in it. I could *find nothing. Then it occurred to me to check on Mrs. Brinker, the widow I believe I mentioned earlier. She and Coombs had apparently been quite close for several months.*

As it turns out, Mrs. Brinker had made certain arrangements. She had rented a cottage in Cornwall in the name of a Mrs. Chesterton, for her husband and herself. How I found the evidence of this, I'd rather not say. But when I confronted her, she confessed that she and Coombs had planned to live in this cottage until they had acquired their share of the fortune from Brayton. Mrs. Brinker insists Coombs never confided how he planned to enact his death. She thought he meant to merely disappear, perhaps leaving a note indicating suicide.

I believe I have come upon a solution. Suppose Mr. Coombs had decided that merely disappearing wouldn't be conclusive enough. He decided a body would be necessary. Then he read Mrs. Reese's article about using submersion to obscure the nature of a murder. He planned to find some tramp about his own age and size, kill him with a blow, and submerge him in the canal. In time, this body would be indistinguishable from that of Coombs. If he left his own watch and jewelry with the body, it would be assumed it was Coombs's. There are several potential flaws with this plan, but perhaps they never occurred to Arden Coombs.

But something goes awry during the execution of the plan. The tramp is able to defend himself and during the struggle, Coombs is bludgeoned. The tramp, knowing his story will not likely be believed, sinks the body in the canal and leaves the district. Since there is nothing else to go on, it may be necessary to leave it at that.

In the meantime, Brayton has laid claim to the tontine's fortune and there seems no reason that he won't receive it in full. If by some chance there is a new development, I will write again.

Regards,
Inspector Reginald Cropsey, Lancs. Constabulary

Again we were left with a mystery to ponder. Though we had no solution ourselves, Harry and I agreed that the Inspector's was most improbable.

The next day was New Year's Eve. In fact, the eve of a new century. The celebrations were elaborate and long-lasting. There seemed to be a sense of optimism that infected everyone. It was while watching the fireworks from the bridge that I came upon my own answer to the riddle of Arden Coombs's death. I once again contacted Mr. Noakes and had him relay a question to Inspector Cropsey. I was sure the answer would be the key to solving the mystery.

While I was giving my attention to the important matter before us, Harry, as was often the case, had spent his time dwelling on some trivial detail. He came home one evening with the air of self-satisfaction he bore all too frequently.

"There are no caves on Long Island, Emmie," he said through a superior grin. "I consulted an authority: the entire coastline of Long Island is flat. You'd be much more likely to find caves along the Hudson."

"I hardly think it likely the subscribers of the *Leek Times and Cheadle News* have such a keen appreciation of the topography of Long Island that they will notice my indiscretion." Of course, Harry had to concede my point and that put the matter to rest.

As they so often do, some of the city's nobles, including the editors of the *Eagle*, had declared a war on vice. The chronicles of their crusade, which had begun the previous fall, provided M.E. Meegs the basis for a whole series of stories. I was handicapped, however, as Harry was too cautious a sort to take me to any of the various "resorts" receiving attention.

I'd been using my winnings from Mrs. Holden's to supplement the household budget, giving Harry the explanation that my remunerations from my work as M.E. Meegs had increased substantially. So I was pleased when Mr. Sackett began sending me clippings of my stories and I had some material evidence of my work. But I was sorely disappointed at how they had been truncated by the graceless editors involved.

It was one evening when we were both at home that we finally heard from Mr. Noakes. That was about the fifth or sixth of February. This was just a couple weeks after the death of Queen Victoria and Mr. Noakes was still wearing a crepe band of mourning. Once again, he came bearing a letter from Inspector Cropsey, which follows:

Dear Noakes,

Please give Mrs. Reese my hearty thanks. Her question proved to be the key and we now have unraveled the conspiracy. I will begin by going back to June of 1898. That is when a Miss Alice Hooper married Arthur Mulvihill, a member of the tontine and a man thought to be quite wealthy. She was his junior by some twenty years. In March of 1899, Mr. Mulvihill's business interests suffered a major reversal. Six months later, he was killed in his home when he confronted a burglar, who was never apprehended.

Though there was evidence that a burglary had taken place, there was also some contradictory evidence. The local inspector had some suspicions regarding Mrs. Mulvihill, but there was no clear motive. They had few assets left at that time and without her husband's income, she was in a somewhat precarious position financially. Afterward, she moved in with a widowed sister some distance away.

Then, as I mentioned in my earlier letter, Mr. Whitley, one of the last three subscribers of the tontine, died of heart failure in March 1900. This left only Arden Coombs and Joseph Brayton.

As you have no doubt already surmised, Mrs. Mulvihill and Mrs. Brinker are one and the same. In addition, I have learned that she visited Mr. Whitley at least twice not long before his death, presenting herself as Mrs. Mulvihill, the widow of his old friend.

She has now confessed to her involvement, but insists that it was all Brayton's scheme from the very beginning. She says he contacted her sometime after her husband lost his fortune. He told her of the tontine and that there were just four members left. Even by her own account, it wasn't difficult for Brayton to persuade Mrs. Mulvihill to join him in his scheme. He then helped her to stage the burglary, and he actually struck the blow that killed Mulvihill.

Later, she says, Brayton provided her with some sort of drug that induced Whitley's heart failure. With Brayton's backing, she then moved to the Rochdale area and contrived to meet Arden Coombs. She was now posing as Mrs. Brinker. She is a woman of just over *forty years, and still attractive, so she had no trouble gaining the attentions of Mr. Coombs.*

Then, she says, Brayton visited her and she showed him the story by M.E. Meegs in her local newspaper. He insisted he would need an alibi, since the motive of the tontine would so clearly direct suspicion at him. He told her she would have to perform the act. She says she demurred, but he threatened to expose her to Coombs, and that would certainly have brought the law down on her, while he would be safe, as he had been careful to avoid leaving any clue to his involvement. Feeling trapped, she did as she was told. She led Coombs on a walk along the canal. When she was sure they were unobserved, she took a spanner from her coat pocket and hit Coombs with such force he was rendered unconscious. Then she filled his pockets with stones and rolled him into the canal, just as Brayton instructed.

Brayton, of course, tells a different story. He says he had never heard of Mrs. Brinker, or Mulvihill, until he received a letter about a fortnight before Coombs's murder, just as he had said earlier. But now he admits the letter came from Mrs. Brinker, saying that there was a confidential matter of mutual concern about which she wished to confer with him. He visited her, as requested, and she laid out the scheme. She would kill Arden Coombs, if Brayton would give her half of the tontine. He says he was shocked at her plan and left immediately. When asked why he didn't report the matter to the police, he gave an unconvincing explanation about the trouble it would cause him.

He says that the day after he read of Coombs's death, he received a visit from Mrs. Brinker, but under a different name. She informed him that she had switched coats with him when he visited her cottage. It was his coat Coombs was wearing when he died. Brayton hadn't noticed any difference, but when he checked, he realized this was the case. He remembered now that during his visit, Mrs. Brinker had contrived to spill something on his coat and took it into another room to sponge it.

He explained that he now felt compelled to go along with her scheme. She provided him the story that it was Coombs who had contacted him and offered a conspiracy, which is the account he gave me originally.

I believe neither account is entirely true. I think it likely that Mrs. Mulvihill acted alone in the murder of her husband, perhaps in the mistaken belief there was more of an estate than there turned out to be. It was at that time she learned of the tontine and that there were just three subscribers left. It seemed out of her reach at the time, but the size of the fortune gave rise to a plan.

She managed to kill Whitley without being detected and then moved on to Coombs. Perhaps her plan was to marry Coombs and then induce him to murder Brayton. But greater familiarity with Coombs's character made her realize that this was unlikely. So she came up with the plan of killing Coombs and either blackmailing, or conspiring with, Brayton. She rented the cottage in Cornwall simply to give credence to her original, false, confession. I believe she was unaware Brayton had put Mrs. Reese's article in his pocket when he visited her cottage, for the article points most to her. She was living near Bacup, whereas Brayton would have been unlikely to come across it. Worthy as it is, the Bacup Times has a limited distribution.

While Brayton may not have been involved in the first two murders, I believe his version of recent events to be false. For one, his alibi for the time of the murder is of the sort that invites suspicion. He was attending a function at his college, in Cambridge, an event he had never attended in the previous forty years. And since he had such a sound alibi, why would Mrs. Brinker's planting of his coat on Coombs's body implicate him in the murder? He could simply say Coombs had visited him and on leaving took the wrong coat.

I asked young Mr. Coombs, the solicitor, if he would apply for the tontine to be awarded to his father's heirs. He said he would, but merely as a matter of principle. He said Brayton has two nephews who are pressing the case that their uncle won it, on the grounds that the tontine makes no provision for situations such as this. Mr. Coombs says their position is nonsense, but that most of the fortune will probably be spent by the trustees during the protracted time the case is argued in Chancery.

Please tell Mrs. Reese that if she ever visits Britain to be sure to stop by Lancashire.

With regards,
Inspector Reginald Cropsey, Lancs. Constabulary

That night we went out as a sort of celebration. Harry was quite generous in his praise, and I reciprocated by pointing out it was the tontine that proved the crux of the matter.

"But what was your question, Emmie?"

"I asked the Inspector what became of Mr. Brinker. I thought that if he had in fact existed, he might have been a member of the tontine. And if he were imaginary, the reason for his invention might provide a solution."

That spring, I was called on to help with the case in which Harry was then involved. And M.E. Meegs took a well-deserved holiday.

Newspaper Clippings

These are the articles authored by Emmie and mentioned in the preceding story which appeared in English newspapers of varying prestige. The copy was taken from what appears to be Emmie's own scrapbook of clippings. You will find photos of it at:

MeegsMorgue.blogspot.com

From the *Bacup Times*:

GRUESOME MURDER IN BUFFALO

The severely deteriorated body of a prominent lawyer of this city was recently found submerged in the Erie Canal. Charles Weigand, Esq., had gone missing in the Spring of this year. Weigand was an avid yachtsman and when his vessel was found disabled and abandoned, it had been presumed by police that he had drowned in a Lake Erie squall. Private investigators, however, had uncovered Weigand's links to a ring of opium smugglers. As a base of operations, the smugglers used one of the towering grain elevators for which Buffalo is noted. The ringleader was the notorious David Lantry, a cunning criminal well known in New York.

Weigand had been brutally murdered in the Spring, after arousing the displeasure of Lantry and the other confederates. His corpse was then submerged for safe-keeping in the canal, at the rear of a concert saloon. Their plan was to allow the body to be disfigured by its long bath, enough so that the cause of Weigand's death could no longer be determined. Then the body would be placed along the lake shore, giving the impression Weigand had died in the wreck of his yacht and that the body had spent the intervening months adrift.

The facts were uncovered when Lantry and his band attempted to collect on an insurance policy taken on Weigand's life not long before the murder.

~~~ ~~~ ~~~

From the *Leek Times and Cheadle News*:

WHITE SLAVERS ROUTED.
SOUGHT IMMIGRANT GIRLS.

NEW YORK, Thursday.—The crew of the white slave ship *Hippolyta*, a schooner of unknown registry, has been driven from the shores of Long Island. Detective Leverton, an operative of the Pinkerton Agency, led members of the Sag Harbor Vigilance Committee in a fierce and prolonged battle against the ruthless slavers.

What made the affair most singular was that the slavers were, just like their captives, all women. They were of dark complexion and spoke in a tongue unrecognizable by their pursuers. All of the rogues escaped capture, but were forced to swim for their maleficent vessel. They left behind many of their weapons and much of their meager attire. Leverton was awarded the slave captain's corset by way of a trophy.

For the moment, the fate of 147 immigrant girls, tempted from the docks and tenements of New York by the slavers, remained a mystery. But while the vigilantes returned to their domiciles, content with having secured their coast, Leverton maintained the search. It wasn't until early the next evening that he heard a chorus of cries from the cliffs above the shore. Scaling the wall of stone, he came to a large cave and in it found the missing maidens.

So exhausted was he, that he spent the night with the grateful gross of girls. The next morning, he carried each down in her turn. A special train brought the freed captives back to their families. One of their number, an orphan by the name of Lele Losinzky, was wedded to Leverton the next day.

~~~ ~~~ ~~~

[Ed. note: Where the remaining stories were printed is not known.]

WAKEFUL PINKERTON OFFERS BELATED HELP.

The great detective, Robert Pinkerton, heir to the firm of insomniacs that bears his name, was caught unaware when his companion, Jacob Worth, had his watch stolen during an outing at Brighton Beach race track. The watch was of great sentimental and monetary value to Mr. Worth, a prominent politician of the Borough of Brooklyn. Though cognizant the turf is most congenial to pickpockets, Mr. Worth no doubt thought he was secure in the detective's company. The discomfited Mr. Pinkerton has vowed to apprehend the culprit, even if it necessitates another fifty years of sleeplessness.

~~~ ~~~ ~~~

VIRTUOSA PICKPOCKET IS ITALIAN COUNTESS.

A pickpocket of unusual skill has been operating in the precincts of Brooklyn for some time and it is only now that police believe they have identified the culprit. The Countess Consuelo Maria de la Salsiccia, well-known at the gaming tables of French resorts, has chosen the City of Churches as her new home.

Police have known of the woman for some time but it was only when she made the mistake of relieving Mr. Edwin Vanderheim of $1800 that she was identified. Mr. Vanderheim is himself a frequent visitor to the casinos of Europe and recognized the Countess at once. However, he did not realize his large bank roll was missing until the next morning and police have been unable to locate the courtly lady as of this report.

This ability to retrieve, empty, and return a man's wallet unnoticed is the hallmark of the Countess's nimble work. A few months past, she deftly made off with the watch and jeweled chain of Jacob Worth, yet left behind in his vest pocket the keepsake photograph that had resided in a locket attached to the chain.

~~~ ~~~ ~~~

CONFESSIONS OF A CO-RESPONDENT.

NEW YORK. —The recent exposure of a divorce mill in this city has yielded the following lurid account by one of the participants, who has given to calling herself Miss Letitia Dare.

"I was born into one of the fine families of Boston, so you will understand my need to remain concealed behind this false appellation. It was through a youthful indiscretion several years back that I was forced to leave my family's protection and learn to fend for myself, in a world much crueler than I had ever imagined.

"Since that time, necessity has forced me to perform many tasks, and make numerous acquaintances, which I would have joyfully avoided had circumstances allowed me. I will leave it to your readers' no doubt able imaginations as to the details of my trials.

"It was through some legal difficulties that I first became acquainted with the lawyer Henry Zeimer. He offered to help me even though I lacked the means to pay for his services. And he did so admirably.

"I soon learned that he did, in fact, expect payment, but through an unconventional means. He explained that he had a woman client who had been much abused by her husband. She wished to divorce him, to save her children as well as herself, but the husband had had no trouble in making this impossible.

"Mr. Zeimer proposed that if I were to make the acquaintance of this husband, and be seen with him publicly, I could free this anguished woman from her prison-like marriage. The plan required that I appear before a judge and give certain testimony that, while not altogether true, was neither complete fabrication. When I met this woman, and saw the genuine tears she shed, and the spiritual bruises she bore, I agreed most willingly to aid her as best I could.

"I played my part with such proficiency that Mr. Zeimer soon brought to me other women, similarly bound to despicable men, that I might free them as well. Then he introduced me to a gentleman who told a tale at least as harrowing as any of the women. He, quite literally, brought tears to my eyes. There was little question that I was anxious to help the poor soul, but I didn't see how I could.

"As was so often the case, Mr. Zeimer came upon a solution. This man would hire me as a private detective. In that role, I would testify to having seen his wife in various liaisons with men of unknown identity. In this way, no one innocent of cruelty would be harmed."

It should be noted that Miss Dare was given a suspended sentence by the judge in the case, while Henry Zeimer was sentenced to ten years in State Prison.

Hidden Booty

by

Robert Bruce Stewart

I

I was delighted, though not surprised, when things ended just as I had told Harry they would. The renown he secured through solving the case of the missing gold would have been capital enough to launch his own agency. But the two thousand dollars the insurers provided him—however indirectly—certainly helped.

In fact, I had done as much to solve the case as Harry. He had found the gold, but I identified the culprits. What's ironic is that I had a difficult time convincing Harry to take the case in the first place. We had arrived in Trouville just a few days before, having made the crossing on the steam yacht *Spoils of the Sovereign*. Harry, with a good deal of help from me, had solved a case of insurance fraud for a man named Koestler. In appreciation, we were invited to join his party for the trip to France.

On landing, Harry and I had expected to leave the Koestler party and go on to Paris. But before we could leave Trouville, I heard about a consignment of gold having been stolen on a French ship that had recently arrived from New York. As luck would have it, one evening at the casino I was introduced to a representative of the insurance company involved in the case. Monsieur Trepanier was quite loquacious on the matter and I wasted no time in suggesting that Harry might be willing to offer some assistance in locating the gold. You see, Harry had recently completed an important treatise on the subject of burglary insurance. However, he hadn't had much practical experience in the pursuit of thieves, so I took the liberty of embellishing his résumé.

M. Trepanier was impressed with my depiction of Harry's career and wasted no time in making an offer. Since Harry's grasp of French wasn't quite up to the task, I accepted on his behalf. It meant arriving back in New York five weeks earlier than we had planned, which of course was disappointing. But due to some unfortunate financial entanglements, our tour was unlikely to be as comfortable as we might have preferred. The fault for that lies with Mr. Koestler. The man was a common card cheat. I suppose I should have expected as much from a man who made his living manipulating share prices. But I should hardly think it naïve for a guest to expect a little honesty at the table of her host. Our troubles were compounded when we discovered that the French casinos are nothing more than shady schemes bent on swindling their patrons. So there was a certain fortuitousness in our learning of the case of the missing gold.

On the 15th of August, Harry, M. Trepanier, and I took the ferry from Trouville to Le Havre, where the steamship *L'Aquitaine* was docked. This was the summer of 1901, just two days before the boat was scheduled to leave on its return trip. On boarding, we were greeted by the first officer, M. Houyvet, a tall, dour man, who escorted us to the captain's stateroom. There we were introduced to Captain Veblynde, an older gentleman with a neatly trimmed grey beard; M. Rollin, the much younger second officer; M. Guenard, the purser; and Mr. Finn, who represented National City Bank, the New York firm that had shipped the gold on *L'Aquitaine's* previous voyage.

M. Trepanier began explaining the situation, but

Harry had a difficult time following, so it was decided Mr. Finn would do so in English. He was a young man who had the assured manner that comes with money and position. He was actually quite handsome, and spoke French with a near-perfect accent. He told us about the precautions taken with the delivery and storage of the gold on *L'Aquitaine*. There had been five iron-bound oak kegs, each holding nine bars of gold. The total shipment was valued at more than $350,000. The kegs were small, not even two feet tall, yet weighed more than 250 pounds each. A length of red tape was wrapped around each keg so that it crossed itself at both the top and the bottom. Then wax seals were applied at the top where the two ends met. The second officer, M. Rollin, had been sent with a representative of the bank to observe the packing of the gold and its subsequent transport from the Assay Office to *L'Aquitaine*. The kegs were then placed in the vault room, to which Captain Veblynde, First Officer Houyvet, and the purser, M. Guenard, each held a key. All this went without incident, as did the voyage to Le Havre.

Once the ship had docked, Mr. Finn came aboard to take control of the gold. He was led to the vault room, where he checked the seals at the top of the kegs, and all seemed in order. Then a most curious thing happened. M. Houyvet came to the room and reported that three gold bars had fallen through the bottom of the trunk of one of the disembarking passengers. Mr. Finn examined the five kegs again, this time checking the seals more closely. He determined that one had indeed been tampered with. A circular hole had been cut into the top, just big enough to allow a gold bar to pass through. Then the hole was blocked back up with a new piece of wood and the area covered by a wax seal nearly identical to that used by the Assay Office. He had that keg broken open and found that it was packed with lead ingots. He then had the other four kegs broken open. Two were likewise packed with lead, while two still held the gold.

"But even lead weighs appreciably less than gold," Harry pointed out. "Wouldn't the difference in weight be obvious to anyone moving the kegs?"

"The gold bars are well cushioned with sawdust, to prevent abrasions," Mr. Finn told us. "By packing the lead tightly, the weight was nearly identical."

"Who was the owner of the trunk?" I asked.

"Mme. Charlotte Yvard," M. Trepanier answered. "She's the wife of a minister in the current government."

Then Mr. Finn added, "The French consider her above reproach."

He told us the theory was that the thieves had randomly chosen her trunk to put some part of the gold in and had had a confederate dockside who would remove it before she reached customs. But wasn't it more likely that her trunk was chosen deliberately? And for the obvious reason that no customs inspector could afford to offend the wife of a minister by rifling through her belongings. I was puzzled why there had been just three bars, as they were really rather small, just seven or eight inches long. But I hadn't appreciated how much the gold weighed. One little bar, we were told, weighed twenty-seven pounds. And as it was, even three bars proved too much for the trunk. Since none of the passengers had gone through customs when the gold was discovered, instructions were given that all their baggage be searched thoroughly. Likewise the cargo, and any of the crew leaving the ship. But no more of the gold was found.

When the captain inquired how he had solved similar cases, Harry hesitated, either because he didn't understand the question or, perhaps more likely, because none of his cases had been even remotely similar. So I took it upon myself to answer, in French. That way Harry wouldn't be tempted to interrupt.

I had great fun inventing several intriguing episodes, and giving myself a prominent role in each. The first involved a similar theft of gold bullion and necessitated our navigating the catacombs beneath Manhattan. Mr. Finn made the unhelpful remark that he had lived most of his life in New York and was unaware of any catacombs. But I didn't see any reason for his ignorance to inhibit me.

"Oh, it's a closely held secret," I told him. "They were created by red Indians, in the distant past, when the isle of Manhatta was ruled by Princess Wali-lanka. Each night she took a new lover, and in the morning slew him. Vultures were allowed to feast on the corpse, and then, when the bones had been picked clean, they were removed to the royal catacombs."

"Did you see many bones?" M. Rollin asked.

"Easily ten thousand skulls," I told him.

"What a bloodthirsty woman," M. Trepanier observed.

"Not really," I said. "She simply bored easily."

"And you found the gold amongst the skeletons?" the captain asked.

"Yes, cleverly shaped to look like bones, femurs mostly, and painted a dull ivory. We had to pick up each one in turn and test its weight until we had recovered all the gold."

I could see the gentlemen were impressed by my account—all but the cynical Mr. Finn. It was partly to assuage his skepticism that I chose a more pedestrian narrative for the second case. This one involved the theft of bonds from a rich man's safe. The type of crime you read about every day. Unfortunately, in setting up the scenario I introduced far too many characters, and the sequence of events was rather serpentine. When I reached the climax, where I apprehended the jilted lover (Angie Yakeley) of the valet (Thomas Godkin) while pretending to be her cousin (Albert Brandt), I found I had left my audience more than a little confused.

"Wasn't Thomas Godkin the fishmonger?" M. Guenard asked.

"No, no, he was the one-legged wheelwright," Captain Veblynde insisted.

"I thought it was his arm that he was missing," M. Trepanier protested.

"Then how would he manage as a wheelwright?"

"Oh, yes. A clever observation, M. Houyvet," M. Trepanier conceded.

"But doesn't that *prove* he was the fishmonger?" M. Guenard asked.

Happily, M. Rollin came to my rescue by noting that only a very shrewd detective could have sorted out such a bewildering set of facts. For the last story, which was also my favorite, I chose a nautical theme. I wanted to show that Harry and I were familiar with crimes at sea. It began in South Africa, where a gang had stolen a trainload of diamonds. They had dressed up as gorillas and disabled the locomotive by pelting it with papayas, thus causing it to slide completely off the tracks.

I explained that Harry and I happened to be passing through Pretoria on our way to an international conference of insurance investigators taking place the next week in Katmandu. Once the insurers of the diamonds learned who we were, they beseeched us to take the case. Reluctantly, we agreed. We set off on camelback in pursuit of the gang, who themselves were now disguised as pygmy headhunters. At Mombasa, they boarded a dhow they had lying in wait. We chartered a similar boat and eventually caught up with them off a small island in the Bahamas. We ambushed them just as they were burying their loot on a deserted beach. The climax was a chaotic battle fought with scimitars and dirks, with both Harry and I doing a goodly amount of beheading. At last, the pirates were vanquished, the diamonds recovered, and the Maharini freed.

"Maharini?" M. Trepanier inquired.

"Yes, did I neglect to mention their abduction of the Maharini of Valparaíso? That occurred immediately after their sacking of Rhodes."

My tales held the Frenchmen in thrall, while Mr. Finn wore a silly smirk throughout, several times grunting his disbelief. Then the captain insinuated his incredulity about my having actually helped Harry as much as I had reported. He used that belittling tone men take on these occasions, when they dress their derision in exaggerated politeness. Harry is very lucky he never makes use of it. I've always imagined that Mrs. Ertel's husband had used the same tone just before she shot him dead. And as I often remind Harry, Mrs. Ertel was acquitted. Well, needless to say, I took offense at the captain's remark and so offered him a wager: I would find the culprits on my own. Naturally, he was compelled to accept my challenge, but only for one hundred francs. I was cheered some when Mr. Finn said he would put up one thousand francs, but there were no other takers.

Later, when Harry and I reached our cabin, neither of us could hide our disappointment. Our quarters on *Spoils of the Sovereign* were both spacious and beautifully outfitted. It was only reasonable that we expected something similar, having been told ours would be a first-class cabin. What we found was more like a storeroom stuffed with some antiquated furniture. But I felt I needed to make the best of the situation, so as not to make Harry feel guilty for my forgoing our tour of Europe.

Due to his rudimentary grasp of French, Harry had missed much of the conversation in the captain's stateroom. I related the few portions I thought it necessary for him to be made aware of, including the terms of my wager—specifically, that I had pledged that we would work independently. He seemed unconcerned, telling me he already had formulated a plan and had every confidence in its success. I was a little miffed at his indifference. It's true that our methods are very different. But, in the end, they usually complement each other nicely. In this case, I don't think Harry appreciated how gullible it was to believe Mme. Yvard was completely innocent. I suspected he was trying to imagine where the gold was hidden, a course I considered all but impossible. The gold would take up only a very small space in what was a very large ship. Besides, it had already been searched thoroughly. I spent the rest of the afternoon recording the fictional cases I had enumerated earlier. They were really quite good and I thought I could make use of them in my writing.

That evening, Harry and I had dinner in Le Havre with M. Trepanier and Mr. Finn. During the meal, Mr.

Finn told us he'd be on the upcoming voyage of *L'Aquitaine* as well, as the bank was transferring him to its Buenos Aires office. Afterwards, while we were strolling along the quay, I took M. Trepanier aside and inquired about Mme. Yvard. He told me that her husband was a minor minister in the government, but he knew nothing else about her. If that was the case, I asked, why were they sure she wasn't involved? It would simply be out of the question, he said. It was only after a good deal of persistence on my part that he confided that M. Yvard's ministry had something to do with chartering insurance companies.

Before we left him, M. Trepanier presented Harry with a one-hundred-franc note. This payment was part of our agreement. You see, I had told M. Trepanier that Harry would take the case for the intellectual challenge alone. It was he who insisted on a token consideration. What I didn't realize, but which Harry wasted no time in apprising me of, was that by accepting this payment, neither he nor I, as his wife, would be eligible for the fifteen-thousand-dollar reward the insurer was offering for the gold's return. Harry's enthusiasm for the endeavor diminished a good deal that evening.

The next morning, I went back into town and found a library, where I was able to learn more about Mme. Yvard and her husband. She had been born Courtois, to a family of some small amount of aristocratic blood. When she married the middle-aged M. Yvard, about eight years before, she was still quite young—a strikingly attractive blonde renowned for her arresting hazel eyes.

That evening we sat at Captain Veblynde's table, where he introduced us to his wife. Mme. Veblynde was making the trip to New York to visit a daughter who'd married an American. It was the eve of our sailing and there were few others on board. After dinner, Mme. Veblynde and Mr. Finn remained in the saloon with Harry and myself, and I suggested some cards. We played several games of whist and when Mr. Finn went off to the smoking room, he was replaced by an American named Smallby. He told us he was a professor of zoology and an authority on shrews. It soon became obvious that Mr. Smallby understood French even less well than Harry, so I took advantage of the privacy their common ignorance afforded and confided in Mme. Veblynde. I told her about my wager with her husband, much to her amusement. She wished me well and offered to help in any way she could. I asked her if she knew anything about Mme. Yvard, from whose trunk the three bars of gold had fallen. She told me she only knew what she'd read in the newspapers and magazines, and all that amounted to was that the Yvards entertained in the grand style and that Mme. Yvard was a very beautiful woman.

After the card game broke up, and both Smallby and Harry went off, I asked Mme. Veblynde about the officers we had met the previous afternoon. She had been acquainted with M. Houyvet, the gaunt first officer, for a number of years, but knew very little about him beyond that he was unmarried. He was always cordial, and got on very well with the captain, but otherwise was an enigma, even to the other officers. M. Rollin, the second officer, she hadn't known as long, but he was just the opposite, very charming and friendly. Also unmarried, he saw himself as a bit of a Lothario. M. Guenard, the purser, was another middle-aged bachelor who'd been with the company a number of years. An efficient man, but something of a dullard.

That night, when I met up with him again in our cabin, Harry informed me that Mr. Smallby was an impostor.

"How do you know he's an impostor?"

"That nonsense he was spewing about shrews being rodents. He knows less about the Soricidae than you know about geography."

"Soricidae?"

"Shrews, Emmie. The shrew family, Soricidae, is within the order Insectivora, not Rodentia. Didn't you learn anything in school?"

Harry is a font of this sort of arcana, most of it as useless as you might suspect. But this bit of trivia would prove helpful to me later.

II

The next morning, the 17th, the remainder of the passengers boarded and we left port promptly at eleven. After lunch there was a gathering in the smoking room that drew everyone's attention, even that of the women forced to remain outside. I was aware that it had become a tradition on the liners for the passengers to form a pool on each day's run, and now Mme. Veblynde informed me of the mechanics of the enterprise. Several dozen slips of paper, each bearing a figure representing some mileage considered by the organizers to be reasonable, were placed in a hat and drawn randomly. They could be purchased for ten francs apiece. Then in the evening, there would be another assembly and each of the slips auctioned to the highest bidder, with half the proceeds going to the original holder of the slip and half added to the common pool. The next day, at noon, the distance of the previous day's run would be posted by a junior officer and the man holding the nearest number collected the pool. It seemed a wonderful opportunity for someone in my circumstances. But it was a men-only affair, and Harry, for no good reason at all, adamantly refused to take part.

That evening, and for the remainder of the trip, Harry and I sat at the table of the second officer, M. Rollin. M. Guenard, the purser, was also there, along with Mlle. Moreau, his fiancée, and a young woman named Julie Dupagnier. *Madame* Dupagnier, she pointed out to M. Rollin, who appeared unconcerned with the distinction. She wore her long, brunette hair in an intricate knot that changed each day. She was clearly attractive, but obscured the upper half of her face with a veil.

Mlle. Moreau was at least as old as M. Guenard, forty-five I would guess, with dark hair, and peasant-like features and figure. She reminded me of my mother, who would have felt equally awkward in the first-class saloon of an ocean steamer. At one point, she mistakenly offered the glass meant for dessert wine to the waiter. A faux pas hardly worth noticing, one would think. But when she briefly left the table, Mme. Dupagnier took the opportunity to make a catty remark about it. M. Guenard turned very red and forgot his position for a moment, telling Mme. Dupagnier she was being rude. But then M. Rollin said she obviously hadn't realized the relationship between the two of them. The purser apologized for taking such offense. I couldn't remember for certain, but it seemed to me we were all at the table when the introductions had been made. I knew Mme. Dupagnier's type very well from college, and my sympathies were firmly with Mlle. Moreau.

The next morning, I asked Harry if he had searched the officers' quarters.

"No, do you think I should?" he asked.

"Surely they are the chief suspects."

"Maybe, but does it seem likely the thief will have the gold neatly piled under his bed?"

"I wasn't suggesting that. But there might be other clues about."

"Ah, clues! Yes, I forgot all about clues. Thank you, Emmie, for reminding me."

I wasn't pleased about having to suffer Harry's sarcasm. But I did achieve my end. Harry spent the day alternately angering and incommoding the officers, to the great detriment of the ship's efficiency. In the meantime, I visited the ship's library, where I was able to verify his account of shrew taxonomy. Later that afternoon, when the men were gathering for the drawing of the lottery in the smoking room, I stopped Mr. Smallby, the faux professor, and led him aside.

"Mr. Smallby, you are a charlatan," I told him. But I made sure to smile, and wasn't at all accusatory. "You know nothing about the Soricidae."

"That's true enough," he conceded. "Who in the world are the Soricidae? Arabs?"

"The Soricidae are the shrews."

"Oh, yes. Those little fellows. Are you a connoisseur of shrews?"

"No, not particularly. But a brief visit to an encyclopedia was enough to verify your fraud."

"Well, no harm's been done," he said. "It was just a little joke."

"I'm happy to accept your explanation. It can remain our secret."

"Thank you, Mrs. Reese. And if there's something I can do for you?"

Of course, there *was* something he could do for me and I wasted no time in telling him. I proposed that we form a syndicate for the purposes of the pool. He smiled, and agreed readily.

"But you haven't heard my terms yet," I told him. "At the auction this evening, we need to acquire the shortest run."

"You think the weather will take a turn for the worse?"

"Yes, something of that nature. However, I must depend on you for the capital."

"I'm not a wealthy man, Mrs. Reese. But I'll make every effort to do as you wish."

That evening at dinner, Mme. Dupagnier made a point of sitting beside M. Guenard, the purser. She was acting peculiarly attentive toward him. I say it was peculiar not merely because she was a married woman, or because his fiancée, Mlle. Moreau, was seated at his other side, but because, whatever positive qualities M. Guenard might have had, charm and good looks were not among them. And Mme. Dupagnier, in spite of once again covering her eyes with a veil, was quite obviously a very beautiful woman. I assumed, at first, she used this to mask some scar or birthmark. But I soon learned that was not the case. A waiter passing too closely behind her disarranged her hat, and I helped her to right it. There was no mark or scar. And had I eyes like hers, I would not be hiding them.

After dinner, Mme. Veblynde and I went to the music room, where several passengers had offered to give a performance. It was really quite excruciating. I wanted desperately to leave, but knew my companion was obliged by her position to endure the spectacle. Meanwhile, Mr. Smallby had gone off to the smoking room to do his duty by the syndicate. When the concert had at last concluded, Mme. Veblynde excused herself and M. Rollin, who'd been seated at my other side, suggested a stroll on the promenade deck. He'd apparently been rebuffed by Mme. Dupagnier and I had moved up on his list. Hoping to gain some intelligence, I agreed. Only later did I realize he'd misinterpreted my enthusiasm. He led me out and as we walked pointed out several constellations of the zodiac. When we rounded a corner, I saw Harry on the deck below. He disappeared down a hatch with a bottle of wine in his hand. The sight gave me an odd, and completely unfamiliar, feeling. I don't think it was jealousy, exactly. But certainly something more than curiosity.

In the meantime, M. Rollin was attempting to ingratiate himself by exaggerating my charms and beauty. It was easy to imagine him chalking up conquests with each voyage. I asked him if he'd made the acquaintance of Mme. Yvard during the last voyage. Unfortunately, my object was all too transparent. But instead of taking offense, he found it very humorous. He told me he had swept her off her feet, but her obsequious devotion quickly became too taxing. He gave her the gold in lieu of his affection, and sent her back to her husband. I laughed, and then told him I needed to go in. He moved quite close and I began to feel not a little discomfited. He told me he had a secret to confide. From the look in his eye, I thought I had a very good idea as to the nature of his secret and told him it held no interest for me. I repeated that I needed to go, as my husband was waiting for me. It was just then that Harry passed not five feet from us, yet took no notice at all. That made it rather difficult to convince M. Rollin he was pining anxiously for my return.

The next morning, Harry was planning to search the crew's quarters and asked me how to politely wake a man and ask to search his belongings. I thought a bit, and then sang out in the lilting voice a mother would use with a child, "*Réveillez-vous, morse paresseux! Laissez-moi voir ce que vous cachez.*"

"*Morse paresseux?*" he asked.

"It's an idiom. It means something like 'my dear comrade.' But the intonation is key."

It took some doing, but eventually Harry was able to speak the lines well enough to convey his intentions. Or, I should say, my intentions. I had misled him, of course, but it was his own fault for being so credulous.

I couldn't be certain what effect he would have, going about calling the crew lazy walruses and accusing them of hiding things, but I assumed it wouldn't be a positive one. At noon, a young officer went to the smoking room and posted the previous day's run. A crowd had gathered, but I feigned indifference. Then, to my relief, I heard Mr. Smallby being congratulated. Many expressed puzzlement that so little progress had been achieved, as the weather had been clear and there was little wind to speak of. As we had arranged, Mr. Smallby kept our winnings until after he had again secured the shortest distance at that evening's auction.

Just after lunch, M. Rollin came off watch and found me speaking with Mme. Veblynde on the promenade deck. She absented herself almost immediately, saying she needed to do some mending. M. Rollin again mentioned his secret, this time adding that it might be an important clue as to the identity of the thieves. I said in that case, I was indeed interested. He insisted he needed to tell me someplace private and proposed using our cabin. I laughed at the suggestion, but he told me he only wanted to aid me in winning my wager with the captain.

"You know something that would expose the thieves?" I asked.

"Perhaps. It's certainly curious."

"Why then didn't you reveal it previously?"

He said it would have seemed as if he were pointing the finger at one man, and he didn't feel sure enough to do that. It had the sound of plausibility, so finally I acquiesced and left for the cabin. He joined me there not long afterward. I had some trouble returning his attention to the clue he'd mentioned, for the man was as persistent as he was charming. But eventually, he told me that on the day the theft was discovered, he noticed that the kegs were sealed with red wax.

"Isn't that normal?" I asked.

"Yes, but when we saw them sealed in New York, I'm sure it was a deeper color. Much darker."

"Well, that would merely confirm they'd been tampered with. Which is obvious."

"Yes, but I believe I had the same feeling when we brought the kegs on board in New York. The color didn't look right. That is what I found curious."

He seemed to be implying that the kegs had been tampered with between the time the gold had left the Assay Office and when it came on board *L'Aquitaine*. But I reminded him that he himself had accompanied it.

"Yes, that is true. But I was not watching it every moment. And the gold was loaded into a wagon, while M. Palmer and I followed behind in a carriage."

"Who is M. Palmer?"

"The representative of the bank, in New York. The wagon was in our sight the whole time, and I saw the kegs unloaded at the pier. But..."

"But if someone had been very clever, and well prepared, they might have switched kegs at some point."

"Precisely. I make no accusation, please understand."

"No, no. Surely not."

M. Rollin's mind now moved on to other subjects. It was becoming increasingly challenging to keep him at bay in the tiny cabin. I had just removed a hat pin and was preparing to plunge it into his thigh, when the steward knocked. At my invitation he entered, acting as if it was quite normal to find a ship's officer in a lady's cabin. Happily, the intrusion was sufficient to send M. Rollin on his way.

At dinner there was an empty seat beside M. Guenard. His fiancée was not feeling well, he told us. We all voiced sympathy, including Mme. Dupagnier. But she took immediate advantage of the situation. And it was clear M. Guenard was coming to enjoy her attentions. Meanwhile, M. Rollin made me the target of his.

That evening, another performance was scheduled in the music room. And this one involved a child prodigy. Mme. Veblynde winced when she told me. I suggested we instead retire to the ladies' drawing room and I would teach her to play bridge. Mr. Smallby came by about eleven. He managed to slip me an envelope containing two hundred francs, the equivalent of forty dollars. I had hoped for more, but assumed he had needed to bid higher at the evening's auction in order to secure our preferred position. It was quite late when I went down to our cabin that night. Harry had preceded me some time before and I saw no one else about—until just as I reached our door. I heard a noise not far away. I turned and distinctly saw M. Houyvet, the first officer, emerging from one of the passenger cabins. The next morning, I discreetly asked the steward who that cabin belonged to. It was Mme. Dupagnier's.

After lunch, I spent some time trying to reach some conclusion about the case. At first, I was inclined to dismiss M. Rollin's evidence, as it didn't explain the three bars in Mme. Yvard's trunk. If the gold had been stolen in New York, there seemed no logical reason for any being in her luggage. But then, I wondered, could that be why it was there? By having the gold fall from the trunk, they made it seem certain that the gold *had* been on the ship. Perhaps Mme. Yvard was the lover of one of the conspirators. She'd been somehow given the gold in New York, and her trunk deliberately weakened.

That night, I had a long and informative conversation with Mme. Veblynde. I was in her cabin keeping her company while the captain was on watch. She told me a most amazing story about the Countess von Schnurrenberger, whom we had seen in Trouville. But since it bears nothing on the present story, I will save it for a later installment.

I slept quite late the next day, missing breakfast entirely. There was a note from Harry telling me he was off making a search of the engine room. Just as I was reading it I heard a great clanking and I had the impression the ship had slowed. When I later asked Harry if the noise had anything to do with his search, he denied it, but then became suspiciously evasive. Harry is a horrible liar. By that I mean he is horrible at hiding his lies—a quality any wife would find endearing.

After I'd confirmed that the syndicate had again been victorious, I went off to look for Mr. Finn. I was anxious to confront him on the matter of the wax seals mentioned by M. Rollin. Just after lunch, I found him in a deck chair reading. He agreed to meet me in my cabin. There, I told him what I had heard about the wax seals. He became very defensive and revealed that Mr. Palmer, the bank officer who had escorted the gold with M. Rollin, was his father-in-law. He seemed to think that would in some way alleviate my suspicion. It was a naïve notion, of course, for it merely made me suspect him as well. Nonetheless, I apologized for upsetting him and agreed there was probably nothing to the rumor. When I showed him out, I saw someone, a man, peering down the passageway in our direction. He moved away quickly, but I felt certain it was Mr. Smallby. I hoped he was coming to give me another share of our winnings, but when I spoke with him later he said I must have been mistaken. Due to our success, the bids at the auction for the shortest run had gone up, and he didn't want to be caught short. I agreed he should continue to hold the money and even returned the two hundred francs he'd given me earlier.

III

That evening at dinner, the purser, M. Guenard, arrived with Mlle. Moreau on his arm. Mme. Dupagnier's seat was taken by a young Canadian gentleman and we were told she was dining elsewhere. I was once again seated for M. Rollin's convenience. How quickly the charming gentleman becomes the bothersome windbag. He suggested we take a stroll after dinner and I consented, chiefly to challenge him on the matter of the changing colors of sealing wax.

"That was a lie you told me, M. Rollin." This was merely a conjecture on my part, but I thought one worth trying.

"Not a lie, but perhaps my memory is not so good," he replied playfully. "But you make it so difficult to see you in private."

"It's for your own safety. I should have warned you how jealous Harry can become."

He smiled at the thought—until I told him how Harry once shot a man who had threatened his position with me, and then hid the body by sinking it in a putrid industrial canal. I had no trouble telling a very convincing story. Not that Harry had ever done such a thing, but I had often imagined he would. I told him I was sure Harry was spying on us at that very moment. But it was only when I alluded to a revolver that M. Rollin finally made some excuse and absented himself. I was quite relieved to be rid of him. But all I had accomplished was to confirm that M. Rollin's testimony about the wax was doubtful, not that Mr. Finn was innocent. It seemed quite a coincidence that the loading of the gold was supervised by his father-in-law.

That night, when we returned to our cabin, Harry found a lady's handkerchief lying just inside the door. He seemed not to realize whose it was, and I didn't see any reason to share with him that I recognized it as Mme. Dupagnier's. She wore a most distinctive perfume. Harry assumed the steward had dropped it there, but why would a steward have Mme. Dupagnier's handkerchief?

I lay awake for some hours trying to reason out who had stolen the gold. Then it struck me. What if Mme. Dupagnier was really Charlotte Yvard, the minister's wife? Suppose she had conspired with some member of the crew to steal the gold and secrete three bars in her trunk. They had been found, but she had come back to make another try. The woman I knew as Julie Dupagnier had hazel eyes, and they were just as stunning as the reports of Mme. Yvard's. The veil was used to obscure them. She must also have dyed her blonde hair brunette. I wouldn't have thought this would be enough to fool the attentive eyes of M. Rollin, but perhaps he hadn't really spent any time with Mme. Yvard at all. And it would explain why M. Houyvet had visited her cabin: *he* was her confederate. She must have snuck into our cabin to find out what we knew.

At breakfast the next morning, I convinced Harry he should begin searching the passengers' cabins. He spoke with the captain and one of the stewards was assigned to accompany us. I made certain that Mme. Dupagnier's was included. If she was spying on us, I thought it only fair that we should return the favor. I must admit to being rather envious of the woman's wardrobe. I'm no slave to fashion, unlike some of my friends who'll impoverish themselves for a new pair of shoes. But I do know the goods when I see them. I was able to confirm that it was indeed her handkerchief we'd found in our cabin. I also found a leather brace. It looked like some sort of orthopedic device. But I couldn't fathom how exactly it was to be worn. And the stitching had been done by a clumsy hand. Then I went to her dressing table and found her brush and combs. I looked carefully at several strands, but, alas, the hair was not dyed.

I had some difficulty in disengaging Harry from Mme. Dupagnier's lingerie, but eventually we made our way to Mr. Finn's cabin. There was nothing at all incriminating among his possessions. Though the nauseating endearments he and his wife used for each other should really never have been recorded, even in private correspondence. She had preceded him to New York, apparently. In one letter, she made reference to the fact that her father was retiring and would be joining them in Buenos Aires.

That afternoon, I showed Mme. Veblynde the handkerchief. She examined it carefully and told me it would have been very expensive, as was the perfume. I then told her who it belonged to, and about M. Houyvet's suspicious behavior. She thought it unlikely there was any association between the two. And while I agreed that there seemed little about M. Houyvet that would tempt a woman to stray, the facts spoke for themselves. I told her that I had already searched the lady's cabin and was determined to search the first officer's as well. I believe I shocked her with this revelation, but ultimately she conceded it was necessary. I asked her if she would accompany me. This she declined to do. She did, however, agree to determine at what time he would be standing watch and, after a great deal of cajoling, to lend me a ring of keys the captain kept in his desk.

My best opportunity would be sometime after the 2 a.m. watch change. At three, I left our cabin without waking Harry and made my way to M. Houyvet's. There was no one about at that hour and I only needed to try three keys before I found the one that fit. I covered the porthole and turned on a light. M. Houyvet was a very neat man, though I suppose that may be characteristic of all ship's officers. The cabin held some family keepsakes, and a number of books. But I saw nothing at all suspicious—until I came across a small casket in the depths of his chest. It held a most intriguing plunder. There were two unmatched stockings, three garters, five pieces of lingerie, easily a dozen handkerchiefs, and a half-dozen earrings, no two alike. I was sitting on the bed with this suggestive collection in my lap, when suddenly the door swung open. It was M. Houyvet, and I can honestly say I'd never been so frightened in my life. I gave a small yelp.

But instead of sounding the alarm, M. Houyvet acted sheepish. I asked him if these were mementos of various conquests. He blushed. No, he said, nothing like that. He confessed he found it challenging even to talk to a woman. But he became easily infatuated with the beautiful women he met on board and had at some point developed the unfortunate habit of removing these souvenirs from their cabins as they slept. He sat down beside me on the bed. Then he picked up each piece in succession and told me about its owner. But not as a gushing romantic. More as the poet Mallarmé would have expressed it. It was quite intoxicating. I told him his talents were wasted, and he blushed again.

He confessed he knew nothing about Mme. Dupagnier, other than that she was so exquisitely beautiful. He'd never even spoken to her. I showed him the handkerchief, but he said he had not taken it. He retrieved a second chest from under the bed and pulled out a beautiful piece of silk lingerie. There was no mistaking that it was Mme. Dupagnier's. He insisted he had no idea how the handkerchief had gotten into our cabin. And I felt he was telling me the truth, having seen nothing of my own in his collection. It seems odd in the retelling, but I must admit that my vanity was wounded when he confirmed that was the case. And I think this sensitive man realized my feelings. He glanced up at the small comb I'd placed in my hair before leaving our cabin. As we sat there, side by side, M. Houyvet reached up and removed it with a delicacy that can only be described as erotic. I was blushing now, and knew I needed to leave quickly. I told him his secret was safe with me and then left him—and my comb.

The next morning, there was a great deal of commotion below decks. There was some trouble among the third-class passengers and it was several hours before the crew finally restored order. Somehow, those in steerage had heard there was gold hidden aboard the ship. Not surprisingly, they initiated a vigorous search. I wasn't sure if Harry was behind it, but whatever the cause, it was very good news for the syndicate.

Later, I returned the keys to Mme. Veblynde. Given that she had taken some risk in the matter, I couldn't very well keep from her what I'd learned about M. Houyvet. She seemed pleased, as if it came as a relief to her that he had some hidden depths. She told me M. Houyvet always took the watch at dinner time and so had had little opportunity of socializing with the passengers. But in the future she would try to remedy that. As I anticipated, she asked if I had found anything of hers among the treasures. She described an earring she was sure had gone missing on board and I told her I'd most definitely seen it.

Harry spent most of that afternoon hanging about the cabin reading. I asked him if he was ill, and he insisted he was fine. It wasn't like Harry to be stoic about such things, but when he told me he expected to spend the next day resting I felt some concern. Then the doctor came by, without us even calling for him. After he examined Harry, I escorted him out. He told me that the ship's officers were convinced Harry wasn't entirely rational, as his searches seemed to achieve nothing other than to disrupt the ship's routine. I suggested it was probably nervous exhaustion.

With Harry's searches suspended, and the captain making every effort to regain some of the lost time, I thought a reversal of strategy was in order. I informed Mr. Smallby that he should bid for the longest mileage. When the time was posted the next noon, we had won handily. I now made discreet use of M. Houyvet's friendship and asked about the prospects for our last day at sea. He said extra stokers had been put on and the weather ahead seemed to be excellent. I suggested to Mr. Smallby that we use our entire capital to acquire the longest mileage again that evening. He made some cautious reply, but given that I knew him to be carrying on some subterfuge, he was forced to carry out my instructions. Later that evening, Mme. Veblynde made a rather startling revelation. I was playing bridge in the saloon when she rushed up and all but dragged me out on deck.

"She's a Courtois!" she exclaimed.

It was some time before I was able to calm her. Then she made her meaning clear: Julie Dupagnier had been born Julie Courtois. I remembered then that Mme. Yvard was none other than Charlotte Courtois. Apparently, she was a younger sister of Julie's father. We both agreed this was just too much of a coincidence. I resolved to keep an even closer watch on Mme. Dupagnier.

The next morning, our last at sea, I came upon a most unexpected sight. Harry had disappeared and I was on my way to breakfast alone. Coming up a stairway, I saw Julie Dupagnier, née Courtois, together with Mlle. Moreau, the purser's fiancée. They were chatting amiably. Then they separated on entering the saloon. How odd that they should become friends, I thought. I began to look for M. Guenard, but was interrupted by yet another commotion below decks. It came as no surprise that Harry was responsible for it. But what *was* surprising was that he'd actually found the gold. Or most of it, anyway. Seventeen bars of the twenty-four still missing. I was dumbfounded. I'd never realized he'd actually been looking for it.

Later, Harry and I were invited to luncheon in the captain's stateroom. In addition to the captain and his wife, Mr. Finn was also with us. Harry, of course, was roundly congratulated. Given that his methods had seemed so haphazard, and his exertions so lackadaisical, everyone was very curious to hear how he had managed it. No one more so than myself. He told us how he had deduced that the thieves must have known a shipment of gold would be arriving on board in New York. So, they arranged for a quantity of lead to be shipped as cargo as well. During the voyage, they cut into three of the kegs, removed the gold, and replaced it with lead. They then planned to smuggle the gold out in the crates the lead had been shipped in, so the theft wouldn't have been exposed until the kegs arrived at the bank in Paris. But once the three gold bars fell out of Mme. Yvard's trunk, they knew the cargo would be searched. So they removed the gold from the crates and hid it elsewhere on the ship.

"But how did you find where they'd hidden it?" I asked.

"I didn't. I couldn't even imagine how to go about that. It seemed far easier to have them bring the gold to me."

"And how did you manage to orchestrate that?"

"First, I made it known among the crew that there would be no need to search the cargo because it would be guarded throughout the trip. Then I arranged to have the same man assigned to that task who had been guarding the gold during the last voyage."

"I see. You thought he must have been in on the theft."

"Either that, or wholly incompetent. I soon found out it was the latter. Give Seaman Francher a bottle of claret and he'd sleep through the Apocalypse."

"And you took him the claret?" I asked.

"Yes, quite a lot of it. I wanted to make it as easy as possible for the thieves to sneak the gold in among the cargo. Then this morning, Seaman Francher and a couple of his fellows helped me search the cargo. Eventually, we found the gold in a large piece of machinery."

I was happy for Harry, of course. But while he was enjoying himself in the role of Holmes, I wasn't content to play his Watson. I was now all the more anxious to solve my part of the affair, for the identity of the thieves was still unknown. The captain suggested that we forget about the wager. And Mr. Finn agreed. They seemed to think they were being chivalrous, but as is often the case with men, the chivalry was just a cloak for the ever-present condescension. Whatever his faults, Harry is never chivalrous. I assured the two gentlemen that there was no need to call off the wager.

"You expect to locate the gold still missing?" the captain asked.

"You forget, Captain. Our wager is that I identify the thieves behind it."

Only Mme. Veblynde seemed to have any faith in my fulfilling my part of the bargain. Just after lunch we reached Sandy Hook, well ahead of schedule. So I was certain our syndicate had prevailed again. We then spent a great deal of time at the quarantine station. Apparently, there had been some illness among the crew and three of them were taken to the hospital there. However, since the technical end of the voyage was the passing of Sandy Hook, I was confident the delay had no effect on our chances of winning the pool.

IV

It wasn't until early that evening that we finally docked in New York. I had made sure that Harry and I were positioned to observe the other passengers as they formed a queue. And I was much relieved when Mme. Dupagnier appeared, listing slightly to one side, then the other. I pointed her out to Harry, but he didn't appreciate the significance—until I reminded him of the leather brace we'd seen in her cabin. Then Mlle. Moreau came into view. She had only a slight slouch, but it was enough to confirm my suspicions. I went over to M. Houyvet, who was supervising the disembarking. I pointed out the two women, but he, too, missed the point.

"The still-missing gold. I believe they may be carrying it. At least a portion of it."

He looked more carefully, and then agreed that the two women appeared decidedly less graceful. He called down to a man on the pier and gave him a message for the customs officials. Then I led Harry back to the captain's stateroom. I had already made Mme. Veblynde aware of my plan and she was there waiting. She told us the captain would be along shortly. Then Mr. Finn, whom I had also summoned, joined us. He asked what it was about, but I suggested we wait. A little while later, the captain arrived. He was impatient, so I revealed that I'd soon be able to identify the thieves. After what seemed like an hour, but was probably just minutes, M. Houyvet appeared. He told me I was correct. The two women had each hidden two bars of gold under their clothing, using harnesses fashioned from leather, like the one we had seen in Julie Dupagnier's cabin. Knowing M. Houyvet's secret, I was amused to see him blush with embarrassment over the details.

"Where is M. Guenard?" I asked him.

He didn't know. Everyone seemed puzzled by my inquiry. Mr. Finn was the first to recover his wits.

"The purser?" he asked.

"Yes, it must be him."

M. Houyvet left us in order to locate M. Guenard. He was soon found in his own cabin, where the ladies had left him bound and gagged. M. Houyvet brought him to the stateroom and he was informed that the two women had been arrested. He then told us the whole story. The plan was just as Harry had surmised, to re-place the gold with the lead, and the lead with the gold. But the purser denied being behind it. He had been used, he said, by Mme. Yvard. She had seduced him, and the plan was hers entirely. It seems she knew of the gold shipment well in advance. And it was she who had arranged for the delivery of the lead and the fabrication of the faux seal. The work of carrying out the exchanges proved more than M. Guenard could manage alone, so he enlisted a steward he had suspected of stealing from passengers' cabins. The man took no convincing. While most of the gold was to be sent to a warehouse, in the guise of lead, Mme. Yvard had taken three bars with her. As insurance, M. Guenard conjectured. She placed them in the false bottom of her trunk. But apparently when the porter upended the trunk to bring it up on deck, the weight of the gold shifted and it fell through a weak point. Hearing of the three bars' discovery, the purser had his confederate remove the gold from the crates in the hold and hide it behind the wall panels of a little-used corridor.

While *L'Aquitaine* was docked at Le Havre, M. Guenard contacted Mme. Yvard. She spoke to him coldly, telling him they must stay apart. He now realized he had been nothing more than a tool to her. If he wished some reward for all his risk, he would need to see to it himself. So he approached Mlle. Moreau. Years ago, they had had an understanding. He told her he had always regretted that they hadn't married. Then he convinced her to travel on *L'Aquitaine* to New York. During the trip, he told her of his predicament. It was his intention to have her hide two bars under her clothing, using the leather harness he'd fashioned. Then, Julie Dupagnier appeared. She knew all about the scheme, from her aunt, and was there to claim a share on her behalf. In order to assuage her, the purser made a second harness and likewise gave her two bars. But he didn't confide in either woman about the other. This was a grave error. Mlle. Moreau saw him visit Mme. Dupagnier's cabin and, out of suspicion, confronted her. But Mme. Dupagnier convinced her she was being used by the purser, who she revealed was the lover of Mme. Yvard. When Harry uncovered the bulk of the gold, M. Guenard lost his nerve and wanted to leave the ship. But the two women were afraid that would give them away before they themselves could disembark with their own gold. So they made him a prisoner in his cabin.

"What about the last three bars of gold?" Mr. Finn asked.

The purser swore he had no idea where it was. His confederate was brought in. With the purser having given him up, he likewise confessed. But he also pled ignorance about the three missing bars. They were taken away and both Mr. Finn and the captain admitted I had won the wager. Mr. Finn had just counted out two hundred dollars—the equivalent to one thousand francs—when there was a knock at the door. It was my associate, Mr. Smallby, accompanied by two New York policemen.

Smallby, it seems, was a private investigator hired by National City Bank. They'd come to arrest Mr. Finn. Apparently, he and his father-in-law had conspired to steal from their employer—not gold, but bonds. They'd been falsifying ledgers for the last few years, moving securities to their own accounts, and eventually accumulating a sizable fortune in South America. The two hundred dollars on the table was seized by the policemen and Mr. Finn taken away in handcuffs.

Mr. Smallby then asked me to join him on deck. He confessed he hadn't been able to secure our desired position in the final pool because he'd been distracted by his investigation of Mr. Finn. So he instead used our capital to make a side bet on what time we would dock in New York. The delay brought on by the bother at the quarantine station caused him to lose the bet and all our money. I was crestfallen. I'd gone to great effort to ensure my fortune, and this man had bungled it. Back inside, the captain paid me the hundred francs that he owed me. While I was glad to have succeeded, it seemed that I had gone through quite a lot for twenty dollars.

Once through customs, Harry and I went off to our apartment in Brooklyn. Since we hadn't expected to be back until sometime the next month, we'd given our maid, Mary, a month's vacation. The larder was empty, and so we went out to a nice restaurant for dinner. When we returned to the Margaret, our building on the Plaza, a French seaman approached us. Harry introduced him as

Thibaut Francher, the undependable watchman. Then two of Thibaut's friends emerged from the shadows. We invited them inside, where they told the most perplexing story of feigning illness so they'd be removed from the boat at quarantine. Then they escaped from the hospital in a dinghy. When I pointed out it seemed like a rather unnecessary detour when they would be arriving in New York shortly anyway, they said something about never getting enough leave. After they had consumed every drop of spirits in the apartment, Harry gave them a portion of our meager cash and suggested they take a hotel room. Since we had two spare rooms, I found this decidedly inhospitable, and not at all like him.

When I asked Harry about his unfriendly attitude, he said that he simply didn't feel comfortable having the truant seamen staying in our home. About ten the next morning, he informed me he needed to attend to some business. This heightened my suspicion. I let Harry go off alone. But five minutes later I set out myself, heading to the hotel which Harry had recommended to our guests. I hid outside where I could see the entrance but would myself remain unobserved. Ten minutes went by before the four of them emerged. Harry led them to a car going across the bridge to Park Row. I just managed to board at the far end. Once on the Manhattan side, they disembarked and walked over to William Street, then down to a building I was unfamiliar with. They took an elevator up to the sixth floor. The doorman informed me that the sixth floor housed a firm of lawyers. Given that they must have gone to see someone Harry was acquainted with, the general nature of this lawyer's practice was obvious. And I could think of no likely explanation for the three Frenchmen wanting to consult such a lawyer, save one:

they had the remaining three bars of gold. Most people don't realize it, but insurance companies aren't at all adverse to dealing with thieves—provided it saves them a sizable amount of money. When Harry came home that afternoon, I told him what I had observed and insisted he reveal all.

"It's not what you think, Emmie. I was as surprised to see the fellows last night as you were."

"But you knew they had the gold?"

"Yes, I did know that. And that they left the boat at the quarantine station."

"Why did you remain silent when you were telling the captain the rest of the story?"

"Well, I had made a deal with the fellows. You see, yesterday morning I woke Thibaut and told him I wanted him to help me search the cargo. He pointed out we'd need tools and went off to find some. He came back with the tools as well as the two other fellows. We opened all the crates, but found nothing. Then they split open some barrels and the whole floor was soon covered in some kind of lubricant. I had a feeling I'd let things get a little out of control, so I tried to rein the boys in. But they'd developed a certain momentum that would have been pretty difficult to stop. Finally, the only thing left was that giant piece of machinery. Some sort of press. It looked formidable, big pieces of cast iron with gigantic bolts holding it together. But the fellows knew its weak points and in no time its insides were exposed. That's where we found the twenty bars hidden."

"All but the four found on the women."

"Yes, all but those four. Well, I was feeling pretty pleased with myself, and the fellows even more so. But the gaiety didn't last long. It seems that my comrades were strongly against turning over the gold. And they made several very persuasive arguments against my crossing them, all of which ended with me being bludgeoned and tossed overboard. I made the usual speech about honor and the law, appealed to their patriotism, etc., but it all sounded a little flat when stacked up against twenty bars of gold. Then I came up with a compromise. They could each have one bar, and I could live to see Brooklyn again. At first, they didn't find my idea terribly appealing. But by then our efforts had roused one of the officers and we could hear him coming down the metal stairway. In a flash, the three of them were gone."

"Then they managed to feign illness at quarantine?"

"Yes, but I imagine it had more to do with some authentic bribery."

"How did they know to come here?"

"I'd given Thibaut our address. We'd gotten kind of chummy. That was before the mutiny, of course. Once they got ashore it dawned on them that disposing of gold bars in a strange city held certain perils. The people who'd be willing to take on the merchandise would be just the sort willing to send them to the bottom of the bay. And, as I said, Thibaut and I had developed a kind of rapport."

"Before the mutiny," I added for him. "And now you've found a lawyer to negotiate with the insurance company?"

"Yes, at least to test the waters. One never knows how these things will transpire."

Harry's prophecy proved more true than he realized. That evening, while he was out entertaining his new friends, two men from the French consulate visited me. It seems there was an effort underway to keep certain names from being associated with the affair. I was told that the present government of France would be needlessly maligned if a minister's wife were linked to the theft. They proposed laying the blame on the purser, the steward, and the purser's fiancée, and forgetting about Mme. Yvard and her niece.

"But we will need your cooperation, Mme. Reese."

"That would be quite impossible," I answered firmly.

"We understand, certainly, there should be some... acknowledgement of your efforts. Perhaps a payment of five hundred dollars?"

"Do you think my integrity can be bought so cheaply, monsieur?"

"No, certainly not. I would never suggest anything so crass. But, as I say, as an acknowledgement.... Perhaps one thousand dollars?"

"Will you release Mlle. Moreau as well? If there is one true victim here, it is she."

"I don't think there would be any objection to that."

Having reached our agreement, they immediately handed me the money. All in cash. Their eagerness to complete the transaction caused me to wonder if I shouldn't have held on to my integrity a little longer. But one can never be sure. If they had called me on it, I might have ended up with nothing *but* my integrity. So I had no regrets. And I have kept my side of the bargain to this very day.

A few weeks later, the insurer reached a settlement for the return of the three bars of gold. They would pay half the value, some twelve thousand dollars. The lawyer took a third of this, but then the three Frenchmen insisted Harry accept an equal share of the remainder for his help—two thousand dollars. I was very pleased for Harry.

And for myself, for now I felt no need to tell him about the thousand dollars I'd received. I had plans for that money, and wished to husband it until I was ready to execute them. In the meantime, Harry rented a little office in Manhattan and went into business for himself. I thoroughly approved, of course. However, I declined his offer of a position in the firm. Insurance investigations can be exceedingly dull work and I would be loath to spend a week in Allentown documenting an excessive claim on a fire policy. Nevertheless, I did intend to take an interest in his work whenever it proved challenging. In fact, I was already lining up just such a case for him, and would soon be ready to let him know all about it.

Psi no more...

by

Robert Bruce Stewart

I

This is an account of a decidedly odd set of events which occurred during the spring of 1902. It involved not one mystery, but four. Or, perhaps more correctly, three mysteries and a conundrum—which was, at first, masquerading as a mystery. I had just finished what I felt was my finest literary effort to date, an account of the famed European jewel thief Madame B_____.

It's no exaggeration, nor mere conceit, to say this was a tale worthy of Dumas. For in addition to filching the gems of noblewomen, Madame B_____ also made off with a good many noble hearts. She quite regularly had dukes, counts, and earls dueling over her fickle affections. And enough baronets groveled before her that her boots need never to have touched the ground—a great convenience during the winter months.

The piece was finished in late February. In truth, it had been completed two weeks before, but the damned parrot that Harry, my husband, bought me for Christmas had managed to eat a good part of my manuscript and left the results on the remainder. However, now restored, my work was at last ready for the publisher.

And had I a publisher there would have been no need to visit Mr. Sackett, of Baily & Sackett, Literary Agency. Mr. Sackett (there was, in fact, no Mr. Baily) had placed some articles of mine in English periodicals the previous year. They had achieved a certain recognition, particularly in the county of Lancashire, and I was sure he would welcome the opportunity of marketing my new work. His office was just at the Manhattan end of the bridge, right on Park Row—the Fleet Street of New York. I dropped my manuscript off with him on a Thursday and returned, as instructed, on Monday. Mr. Sackett had read my piece and pronounced it a masterpiece, though perhaps not in so many words.

"Then you think you can find a publisher? *The Strand*, possibly?" I asked.

"Yes, possibly. But what the magazines most want are serials, something that entices the reader to buy the *next* issue. Then, later, we can find a book publisher."

"Oh, I already have plans for just such a book, *The Queens of Criminality*. It would serve as a companion to Lady Carbury's *Criminal Queens*. I was imagining that each profile would appear sequentially in some magazine of note."

"Ah, an admirable aspiration," he said. "But the key to a successful serial is that no installment be finite. For instance, the Madame B____ piece should end with the hint that her true identity will be revealed at the beginning of the next installment."

"But I don't reveal her true identity."

"Quite. However, you do know it?"

"Yes, but I'm pledged never to reveal it."

"Mrs. Reese, if you wish to get anywhere in this game, you must be willing to make compromises. I'm sure your promise was sincere when you made it, but circumstances change."

"It isn't merely a matter of honor. If I were to break my word, I would fear for my safety, and yours, Mr. Sackett."

I knew he thought I was being overly dramatic, but if I'd related to him the truth of Madame B____'s nature, I felt sure he'd want nothing to do with my project. Finally, he suggested that the piece end with the promise that the great woman's identity would be revealed in the next installment, and that we leave off worrying about the resolution until the time came. I agreed, and told him I would begin work on the next queen of criminality. My intended subject was Sophie Lyons, the notorious black-mailing seductress of the previous century. Much had been written about Mrs. Lyons, so I only needed to liven it up with detail and color to come up with my next installment.

Just a week or so after visiting Mr. Sackett—having finished a wonderful, if somewhat fanciful, portrait of Mrs. Lyons—I found myself at loose ends. One Sunday afternoon, for want of something more purposeful, I attended an outing organized by a fellow alumna of my college. Like myself, the others were all recent graduates. And then there was Fanny. Fanny Baum had entered with my class back in '95, but after a year of struggle—during which she had learned little beyond the fact that Latin and Greek were two separate and distinct lan-guages—Fanny surrendered to the inevitable and gave up her academic ambitions. However, she found college life quite agreeable otherwise. She persuaded her very wealthy father to make arrangements of some sort so that she was allowed to stay on in one of the houses. She was given some silly title, "social coordinator," I believe, but no real duties. Fanny attended chapel every morning, sang with the glee club, and kept herself popular by hosting innumerable bunny parties. Bunny being Welsh rabbit, as ambrosia to the gods to college women of my era.

We were taking a cruise up the Hudson and on the

way back Fanny more or less forced her company on me. We had known each other only remotely in school. I didn't even know her real name, nor did I ever see any reason to learn it. Fanny seemed such a fitting moniker for one so thick-headed.

"Did you know I'd married?" she asked.

"No. Congratulations, Fanny."

"Oh, it's over now," she said without emotion. "I hear you live out in Brooklyn, Emmie."

"Yes, we have an apartment just above the park."

"I heard it's a rather large place."

"Certainly for the two of us," I told her.

The conversation proceeded in this desultory way until Fanny confided that her interest in our living arrangements was motivated by the fact she was not getting along with her father and hoped to find temporary rooms until she could set up house for herself. I didn't like the manner in which she had maneuvered me into offering her accommodations, but I did so nevertheless—for three reasons. First, we did have a large apartment with two bedrooms sitting empty. Second, Harry was out of town quite a bit of the time and Fanny, whatever her faults, did offer diversion.

But the primary reason was *Psi*. This was a literary journal of her former husband's which she had taken possession of in the divorce settlement. Actually, it was the mere conception of a journal. It was meant to be one of the little magazines, like *The Chap-Book*, or *The Lark*. But the staff had never managed to publish even a single issue.

"Was it a matter of money?" I asked.

"Oh, we had plenty of that. Or too much. My husband and his friends spent so much time discussing the thing—over endless dinners and what they called symposia—that they never had time left for working. He told me there was no use starting the thing until they had the decadence down pat."

"But then what is it you have?"

"Oodles of paper, mostly. In a warehouse somewhere. And there's a cute little hand press."

On hearing this, I issued an immediate, and most gracious, invitation. This was the answer to any writer's dreams: a press, plenty of paper, and a wealthy dupe living in the next room. With these three things, I would be released from the tyranny of publishers and their petty demands. Still, there was one small matter of concern. What Fanny had neglected to mention was the reason for the disharmony in her father's house. That would be Fanny's manservant, Michel.

Formerly her husband's valet, Michel was another of her prizes from the divorce. It was unremarkable that her father had objected to the arrangement. A young woman with a man acting as her chambermaid invited rumors. And when the woman was as well known as Fanny for her many infatuations, and the servant as pleasing to the eye as Michel, the rumors quickly progressed to scandal. But this bothered me little. My sights were on *Psi*.

A week after Fanny's moving in, I received a letter from Mr. Sackett asking me to come see him at my earliest convenience. I fairly brimmed with anticipation and left immediately for his office. While I was all for freeing myself from the tyranny of publishers, I saw no point in spurning what might be a generous offer.

"I take it you've found a publisher? Is it *The Strand*?"

"I'm afraid that's not the case. Do sit down, Mrs.

Reese." I did so and he resumed. "Yesterday I had a very troubling visit. It was the Marchioness of Karpolov. She objected strongly to your depiction of the marquis and has threatened legal action if your story is published."

"But there is no Marchioness of Karpolov," I told him.

"Well, perhaps the marquis has married recently."

"But how could she have learned of my story?"

"I've sent it to several publications. I imagine some editor is an acquaintance."

He was adamant that he could not afford to proceed without a written agreement from the marchioness and her husband. I left, all the more pleased I had begun preparations for resurrecting *Psi*.

Thus began the first mystery. You see, although Madame B_____ did exist, and we were well acquainted, my account of her life was largely fictional. This was at her own request. The Marquis of Karpolov, Europe's greatest lover since Casanova bounced his way from bed to bed across the continent, was nothing more than an invention of my imagination. Quite a good one, to be sure. But purely fictional nonetheless. Or so I thought. Of course, if there were a real Marquis of Karpolov, I could see how the marchioness would object to my depiction of her lord. I suppose all writers encounter this problem sooner or later, but I'd only been writing a year or two and this was my second time. The first involved a Pinkerton with what I thought was the unlikely name of Leverton. But that's a story that has already been told.

Harry arrived home that evening and it was obvious he wasn't pleased to find we had guests. Then when he learned the parrot had chewed his slippers into a pulp, he almost lost his temper. I pointed out the bird was his gift, and so he merely brooded. Harry had named the parrot Telemachus and told me he'd trained it to repel suitors in his absence. Not that there were any suitors to repel, but I was flattered at the thought.

Harry had to leave town again two days later, which was just as well. A certain friction had developed between him and Michel. This was partly because Harry insisted on calling him Michael. And that, Michel insisted, was an insult to his Parisian heritage. Of course, I knew by his accent he was Quebecois, and had probably never been closer to Paris than Providence, Rhode Island.

For Harry's part, the hostility was due to his new-found jealousy. This was ironic, because Michel seemed to take no interest in me at all. And on the only occasion when a man did show some interest in me, aboard a French steamship the previous summer, Harry had been completely oblivious. When he saw Michel feeding Telemachus, he complained that his flank had been turned, and insisted Fanny and her man be out of the apartment on his return. Then he stormed off to Wilkes-Barre to investigate a fire insurance claim. (Harry's business is insurance fraud.)

I now turned my attention to *Psi*. You are probably wondering why its creators chose such an odd and phonetically imprecise name. As Fanny explained it, this was exactly the reason they had chosen it: No one could read it without wondering if there were some deeper meaning behind it. So, rather than risk exposing their ignorance, they would pretend amusement at the cleverness of it. And no one could utter it without having to explain it. This would always end with a calculated grin, by which the speaker made clear the meaning should be obvious to any save the most obtuse of philistines. It was, in sum, the perfect choice for a literary milieu more noted for its affectation than its talent. To Mary, our maid—an intelligent if uneducated girl—it was always *Sigh*. A beautiful name, she thought.

The next day, Fanny and I visited the warehouse and did an inventory. There was more paper than we could use in a hundred years. And a very nice hand press with many boxes of type. I had these, and a good quantity of paper, delivered to our apartment and placed in the bedroom assigned to—but rarely used by—Michel. Mary had been taken aback when she learned what was going on between Fanny and her servant. She feigned pious offense, but again it was simple jealousy. The poor girl somehow imagined she had captured our resident Don Juan's eye. And though he may have made some flirtatious forays in her direction, his main force was laying siege to his mistress's fortune.

II

My head teemed with ideas for articles and essays which could be used in *Psi*, all written by myself. But what of the graphic element? All the little magazines employed distinctive illustrators who added a much-needed visual dimension—an area of expertise I had no aptitude for. I decided to consult Mr. Sackett and see if he could offer any advice. One morning, Fanny and I found him at his desk reading, so engrossed he hadn't noticed our entrance. I gave a little cough, and he quickly stuck his book in a drawer and leapt to his feet. Red-faced, like a little boy caught smoking, he stammered an apologetic greeting. I introduced Fanny and told him all about *Psi*. Then I asked if he knew how one went about hiring an illustrator.

"What sort of illustrator?"

"One with erudition and wit, able to capture the spirit of the age, and at the same time lampoon it."

"Oh, artists of that sort are in great demand, Mrs. Reese. What sort of budget have you set for illustrations?"

I turned to my companion. Fanny was taking scant interest in the conversation, looking at herself in a little hand mirror she always had with her.

"We'll pay whatever the market demands. Isn't that right, Fanny?"

"If you think we should, Emmie."

"One other consideration, of course, is the cost of printing," Mr. Sackett pointed out. "What press are you working with?"

"Oh, we've a hand press," I told him. "We'll be printing it ourselves."

"Umph. Very arty, but that makes it difficult to accommodate the modern method of printing illustrations."

"Well then, what did they use previously?" I asked.

"Wood-blocks, usually. The artist would make a drawing and the carver would create a printing block. A very involved process, and one that would prove quite expensive now. However..." He began leafing through papers on his desk. "Yes, here it is. An auction of abandoned goods is to be held at ten o'clock this very morning at a warehouse on West Street. 'Among items of interest are seventeen boxes of wood-blocks, formerly used by well-known illustrated magazines.'"

What serendipity, I thought. Out of seventeen boxes we'd be certain to find any number of interesting images. I took the sheet he handed me and prepared to leave. But Fanny had other ideas.

"What was that book you were reading when we came in?" she asked Mr. Sackett.

"Book? Oh, just something a friend sent."

"Let me see it," she demanded

"I don't think it would interest you ladies." He'd turned scarlet again.

"*Let... me... see... it....*"

As I've already noted, more often than not Fanny's limited faculties made her agreeably suggestible. But there were times when her feeble-mindedness was compromised by her willful nature, which was that of a spoiled child. In these instances, to stand in her way required grim determination. And it was soon obvious that Mr. Sackett was sorely lacking in grim determination. Fanny pushed him aside and opened the drawer in which he had hidden his book. When she found it, she stood there reading for a time, then fell into the chair recently vacated by Mr. Sackett. She had also taken on his facial hue. At this point in the proceedings I was torn. On the one hand, I certainly did not want to seem as ill-bred as my companion. On the other, I was dying with curiosity. After a brief skirmish, during which my dignity fought gallantly, if only fleetingly, I began reading over Fanny's shoulder. It was a book of Limericks, but not of the type Edward Lear had made famous. Much as I would like to share with you the content of that little book, I find myself incapable of putting down the words. One told the story of a young lady of Diss, who went down to the river to do something unmentionable. Then a man in a type of boat popular in England and maneuvered by a pole arrived and did something even less mentionable.

"Mr. Sackett!" I ejaculated involuntarily.

"It only just arrived—I'd no idea of the nature of it until I read it myself," he pleaded. "Of course, I will destroy it at once."

"Destroy it?" Fanny asked incredulously. "You'll do nothing of the sort."

She slipped the small volume in her bag and made her way to the door.

"Come along, Emmie," she said. Then nodded toward the clock. "We'll be late for that auction."

In the brief time she'd been staying with me, I'd had ample opportunity to experience Fanny's forthright manner. But her sudden cognizance of temporal constraints caught me unawares. Up until that moment, she'd given no hint she knew what a clock was. I had every intention of insisting she leave the book behind, or that we destroy it ourselves right then. But there was truth in what she said. The auction was due to start in five minutes. I took leave of Mr. Sackett—briskly, and with all due opprobrium. And then we went out and hired a cab. I didn't speak much during the ride, still shocked at what had occurred in Mr. Sackett's office.

Fanny felt no such restraint. She took out her prize and began reading aloud. I protested, of course, but she went on. She had just finished the tragic and quite indecent tale of a young lady of Tring who had positioned herself too close to a fire and injured a particularly sensitive part of her anatomy when we arrived at our destination. The look on the cabman's face suggested he had overheard Fanny's recitation, and the wink he sent our way more or less confirmed it.

"What an insolent man," Fanny said as we walked away.

Though we were but a quarter of an hour late, the auction was nearly completed. I inquired of one of the men running the affair as to the status of the wood-blocks.

"Oh, the man with the missing toe bought them. Already carted them off."

"How much did he pay for them?" I asked.

"Six bits."

I was sick with frustration. I would have been happy for Fanny to pay a hundred times that amount. I decided the thing to do was to find the man with the missing toe and simply buy the blocks from him. But all anyone knew of the man was that he was some sort of seaman, and was missing a toe. This was my second mystery (the first, if you've already forgotten, being the true identity of the Marchioness of Karpolov).

"Does he walk with a limp?" I asked, casting about for some small clue.

"No, not as I noticed."

"Then how do you know he's missing a toe?"

"Cuz he said so. First time we met. Brings it up all the time."

It seemed absurd he would know the seaman was missing a toe but not his name, or where he hailed from. But he then offered some hope.

"He's been coming to all the auctions last few weeks. You come by Monday—we're doing a bankruptcy over on Leonard Street. I'll wager he'll be there."

"Will you be auctioning more printing blocks?"

"No, just furniture."

"What sort of things does this man buy?"

"Anything made out of hardwood."

"To do what with it?"

"Burn it, I imagine."

"Burn it? Why would he pay money just to burn it?"

"For heat. There's a strike at the coal fields. Don't you read the newspapers?"

I nearly fainted. My only hope was that the nine-toed seaman had sufficient fuel reserves—exclusive of the wood-blocks—for the next two days. To make use of the time, and to occupy my mind, I decided to begin work on the content of *Psi*. I had several little pieces already written, but all were adventure stories, and I worried the issue might seem too homogeneous.

Then I remembered my friend Elizabeth's letter from Bangkok. She had taken a position as governess for a Siamese official's two daughters a few months before. In her letter, she described the city and its inhabitants in some detail. I thought it might prove alluring to have a "Letter from Bangkok" in each issue.

Oddly, the letter was decidedly uninspired. I say oddly because Elizabeth could be a very engaging correspondent, and all who knew her esteemed her keen wit. Or, more truthfully, esteemed it and feared it in equal measure. For to be her target left an indelible mark. Yet the letter before me was written in the dry monotone of a school book. I resolved to liven it up some and went off to the Astor Library to do some research of my own. And that gave birth to the third mystery. You see, I did find just such a book as I was looking for: *Siam, the Land of the White Elephant*, by George Bacon. And as I read the chapter on Bangkok, a feeling the French call *déjà vu* came over me—I had read this all before. I paged through Elizabeth's letter, and there was no question—she had merely copied passages from this very same book. Now, if she were in Bangkok, why would she need to use such a source? She wouldn't, of course. Yet the letter was written in her hand, and had been mailed from Bangkok. As I closed the book and rose from the table, a second sensation of *déjà vu* came over me. This one of an aromatic nature. When I had last seen Elizabeth, that previous December, she had taken to wearing a very expensive French perfume. I suppose there were plenty of well-to-do women in New York who might likewise partake of it, but what were the odds that one of this select group would be in the Astor Library consulting Mr. Bacon's book? Long indeed.

Despite the deficiencies of Elizabeth's faux missive, I was determined that the "Letter from Bangkok" would remain a regular feature of *Psi*. It sounded so wonderfully exotic. But rather than plagiarize the book, I would take advantage of the freedom allowed me by my friend's deceitfulness and leave the details to my imagination. Signing the column in her name, of course. I was happily immersed in this task until it was time to attend the auction on Monday morning.

Fanny and I arrived well in advance of the proceedings. No seamen—with or without the full complement of toes—were about, but the wares included a great deal of flammable material and I saw that as a hopeful sign. Then, just before the bidding got underway, he appeared. A man of about forty, though perhaps younger if he'd had a trying time at sea. He wore a beard and a blue seaman's cap. He looked about some, but after the first few items went for many times his modest bids, became disheartened. Apparently these tables and dressers were too fine to be affordable as fuel.

A little while later he left for the street and we followed. I had decided that rather than approach him immediately, we would dog him stealthily and thus learn the location of his lair. That way, if he refused to sell us the wood-blocks we might still acquire them through other means. He went to Park Row, crossed the bridge in a street car, and then switched to the Fifth Avenue L. We managed to make the same train, just two cars behind him. At Ninth Street, he got off the train and walked east. Again, we followed, and were soon crossing the bridge over the Gowanus. There we came upon a throng of spectators looking down at the canal. Fanny wanted to stop, but I was unwavering in my quest.

"They said there's a body down there, Emmie," Fanny said wistfully as I hurried her along.

I looked back over my shoulder and sighed. "Probably just someone who fell in by accident," I told her.

The nine-toed seaman went to the east a block or

two, then south several more. Then he entered a saloon, and not one of the class that sports a family entrance. It was some time before he came out again, and the only way I could keep Fanny amused was to have her read to me from the book she'd confiscated. She read a Limerick—"Nursery Rhymes," the book called them—that centered on the Marquis of Landsdowne. A mere braggart, and not at all like the Marquis of Karpolov, who used his gifts selflessly.

At last the seaman emerged. It would have been easy enough to approach him then, but I surmised we must be nearing his domicile. Again he walked east, and then south. We were in a neighborhood that was completely foreign to me, full of rough buildings and rougher-looking people. Eventually, we came upon the warehouses and docks that line Brooklyn's waterfront, and then to a little inlet. The shore here was pure mud, and sinking into it were the rusting and rotting hulks of several old boats. The seaman approached one of these, perhaps the most decrepit-looking of the lot. It was an old sailing vessel lying on its side. He entered a door fashioned from scavenged boards he'd placed over a hole in what would have been the deck if the boat were properly oriented. We followed as far as the door, but then froze. After a few moments, I overcame my apprehension and knocked.

III

The door opened and the man with the missing toe poked out his head.

"So you came all the way, did you? I thought I lost you a ways back."

"You knew we were following you?" I asked.

"Well, I didn't think you lived out this way. What's it you want?"

"Do you remember purchasing seventeen boxes of printing blocks at an auction on West Street?"

"I most certainly do—they were well received," he said. "But no sense standing there in the mud. Come on in and sit yourselves down."

I followed him in and, rather than be left outside alone, Fanny joined me. As you might guess, it was a decidedly odd room. Larger than I expected, and not nearly as dark. He had placed windows over various openings along the curved ceiling which acted as skylights. He had us sit down at his table while he started a fire in an iron stove. Then he went about lighting a number of lamps. With the additional light, one could see he had made himself a very comfortable home. To overcome the curvature of the boat's hull, he had built little stepped tiers. The floors of these were covered with old, but still attractive, Persian rugs. The furniture was likewise old, but all cherry, and all of a matching patina. The end of one tier was the kitchen and the other end the dining room, where we sat. Above that was a tier devoted to his extensive library. Shelves covered the walls, with additional books stacked on the floor. I don't think I've ever seen a personal collection of such dimension.

"Coffee, or perhaps tea, ladies?"

"Coffee would be lovely," I told him.

"You wouldn't happen to have any brandy?" Fanny asked. "My feet are damp and I'm afraid I'll catch a chill."

"I do indeed, madam. I do indeed."

He fetched a bottle and three brandy glasses of fine cut glass. Then we joined him in a toast to our mutual health.

"We greatly appreciate your hospitality, Mr...?" I began.

"Captain George Ingalls, at your service."

"Were you captain of this ship?" Fanny asked.

"No, alas. I am a landlubber. My title is an honorific, bestowed upon me by my fellows in Coxey's Army."

"So it wasn't a shark that bit your toe off?"

"No, indeed not. I lost it while leading my men on a raid of the Baltimore & Ohio's yard at Cumberland, Maryland."

"Why were you attacking Maryland?" she asked. "Was this the Civil War?"

"No, this was back in '94. Ours was an army of the unemployed, on its way to Washington to seek relief."

"Then why were you attacking Maryland?" she persisted.

"We were not attacking Maryland per se, but rather a boxcar we had reason to believe was carrying a consignment of canned beans, which happened to be located in Maryland at the very same moment we were. You see, my company had missed the rendezvous with the main body of the army, arriving as we did some eight weeks late. That was on account of the rampant lethargy that ran in our ranks. And by then our rations had long since given out. So I thought by launching an attack on that boxcar full of beans, I could kill two birds with one stone. There's no better antidote for lethargy than the sting of battle. Or so I reasoned."

"Did you get any?"

"Beans or relief?"

"Either."

"No, ma'am. My men faltered in the heat of battle, I'm ashamed to say. And, to add insult to injury, or perhaps it should be the other way around, I had failed to realize that the boxcar was in motion. I never got closer to Washington than the Cumberland hospital. The sad truth is that all I have to show for the campaign is my missing toe. I wear it as a badge of honor."

"You wear this severed toe?" I asked.

"I was speaking figuratively, ma'am. What became of the toe itself is a mystery to me."

"I see. Well, as I was saying, we greatly appreciate your hospitality, Captain Ingalls. But we come on a pressing matter."

"Yes. The print blocks. Whatever do you want them for?"

"Well, to print, of course. We are endeavoring to launch a publication...."

"Might I have another glass of brandy?" Fanny interjected.

"Yes, of course." The captain refilled her glass and from that moment made sure it was never empty long.

"We are endeavoring to launch a publication," I continued. "And those print blocks would be most helpful. We would like to purchase them from you. At a reasonable profit, of course."

"A reasonable profit?" he asked.

"Oh, it doesn't need to be terribly reasonable," I said.

"Reasonable or not, I'm afraid I no longer have them in my possession."

"Then who does?"

"Well, if there are any left, the canal boatmen."

"The canal boatmen?"

"There's a whole little city of them, laid up in the Erie Basin for the winter. And with the coal strike on, they'd nothing to burn in their stoves. So I've been providing them what I can."

"That's very admirable of you...."

"Nothing admirable about it, just business."

"Isn't it possible some remain unburnt? It's only been two days."

"Oh, very possible. But I sold them dockside there, and I really don't know which boats they went to."

"You mean they live on the boats?" Fanny asked.

"It's their only home. The whole family travels up and down the canal. Then in winter, when it closes, they come down the Hudson and tie up here. It's the only time the kiddies get to go to school."

"How many boats are there?" I asked.

"Oh, maybe a hundred. Maybe more."

"Would you be willing to visit them and ask about the blocks?"

"No, I'd feel sort of queer about that. I mean, not having anything to replace them with. And I have my studies to attend to." He waved a hand towards his books.

"I see. Well, can you direct us to the Erie Basin?"

"Oh, it's just around the corner."

He took out a pencil and found a scrap of paper, then drew a little map for me.

"Well, thank you again. Shall we be going, Fanny?"

"Fanny? What a beautiful name," the captain asserted.

"Do you think so?" his mark asked coyly.

"Yes, it's easily approachable, yet poetically suggestive."

Fanny just giggled.

"Perhaps Fanny could remain here, and then you might pick her up on your return?" the captain suggested.

I saw no point in debating the matter, and so agreed I would come back for her after making inquiries of the canal boatmen. The captain helpfully provided me with a canvas sack in which to carry any blocks I could acquire and I went on my way.

The Erie Basin is a sort of harbor enclosed by a long wharf and a breakwater. And as the captain said, a good part of it was taken up by canal boats tied one to another in a great mass. To get to them, I needed to go out along the wharf. And this was occupied by a variety of boat builders, warehouses, and saloons. As you might imagine, it wasn't a pleasant walk for an unescorted woman. But I was determined to see this through.

I was skeptical when the captain told me there were a hundred canal boats moored here, but it was no exaggeration. I started at one corner and worked my way along, switching back at the next row. It was wash day, and a great deal of careful maneuvering was required to navigate through the brightly colored laundry which was strung the length of nearly every boat. The denizens were generally friendly, and I encountered quite a number who had bought blocks from the captain. But only a few remained unconsumed. These I was able to procure for two or four bits apiece. I was so excited at my success in finding any that I paid little attention to their subject matter.

Several women invited me to their cabins while they checked for the blocks and I was greatly impressed by their ingenuity. The cabin, no larger than the bedroom Harry and I shared, was the family's kitchen, dining room, and bedroom. One woman told me that she, her husband, and her five children occupied theirs. But even she found room for a few potted plants. And there was always some sort of art up on the walls, mostly yellowed illustrations from newspapers and magazines. The children I met on the boats all shared their parents' colorful language. Profanity came easily to them, but so did geniality.

I rounded the last turn and had just a half dozen boats left to visit when I came to Mrs. Stanton's. Not only had she bought some of the blocks, she told me, but there was still one remaining. We went down where she had mounted the block above a bunk. It told the sad tale of a procuress tempting young girls into her web of immorality. In one scene, the fur-bedecked lady offers the ragged girls coins. Then above we see their future—a scene of gay abandon in the company of men and wine. She told me she had bought it to illustrate a lesson for her daughter. Realizing the value she placed on it, I made her an offer of five dollars. She was shocked at this, and I believe it made her suspicious that the block had some hidden quality that rendered it particularly valuable. She insisted I have lunch with her while she thought over the matter. I was famished and tired, and so accepted her kind offer.

During the meal she told me a great deal about herself. She was a widow and, quite unusually, captain of her own vessel. Her two children, who were attending school at the time, were her sole crew.

"It must be terribly difficult, running your own boat."

"Well, I have to hire drivers for the mules once we reach Troy."

"What sort of things do you haul?"

"Lumber, mostly, from Whitehall and Champlain, up that way." Then she lowered her voice. "But sometimes I have more interesting cargoes. I do some work for these Chinese gentlemen."

I took that to mean she was smuggling items brought over the Canadian border, and only one item came to mind.

"Opium?" I whispered.

"Oh, no, dear. Not opium!" She laughed at the thought.

"Then what?"

"Chinamen!"

"Oh, I see. Because they can't come here properly."

"That's right. They've been excluded. Very unfair, isn't it?"

"Yes, it does seem rather arbitrary."

I was very glad to have met Mrs. Stanton, for I expected a story based on her life would one day find its place in *Psi*—with the names changed, of course. By the time we'd finished eating, she no longer seemed suspicious of my motives vis-à-vis the wood-block and accepted my offer. I imagine this development was due more to her having revealed her smuggling activity than to any argument on my part. It's an odd trait of human nature that we instinctively trust those we've first made privy to our secrets—when it should be the other way around. As I bade her farewell, she admitted her plan for moral guidance had back-fired. Her daughter asked where she could find this nice woman who would pay her to have a good time.

Only when I returned to land did I do a true appraisal of my haul, and, with the exception of Mrs. Stanton's contribution, it was quite disappointing. I had one corner of *The Battle of Chickamauga*, a portrait of Edward J. Phelps (though no explanation of why he was worthy of the honor), a cartoon of a demure woman shielding her face with a fan, another of two peculiarly dressed women dancing together, and several depictions of various kitchen implements. Not the sort of thing Mr. Beardsley provided the *Yellow Book*. However, I did take comfort in the fact that my portion of the battle scene showed a fallen soldier and might be used to accompany one of my adventure stories.

When I arrived back at Captain Ingalls' to gather Fanny, I found them still seated at the table, the drained bottle of brandy between them. Both seemed to be in some sort of reverie, and neither noticed my entrance. They were having a literary dialogue. First, Fanny would read a selection from her book of Limericks, and then the captain would recite something of Shakespeare's from memory. One I recognized as being from *Love's Labour's Lost*:

"From women's eyes this doctrine I derive.
They sparkle still the right Promethean fire.
They are the books, the arts, the academes
That show, contain, and nourish all the world...."
Fanny's reply—involving an impoverished young

woman of Norway, whose unmentionable livelihood was threatened by the unmentionable habits of an unnamed viscount—struck a decidedly discordant note. To my ears at least. The captain seemed enraptured by it. I began to feel like something akin to a voyeur and made a little cough. Fanny blushed on seeing me and quickly came to her feet.

"There you are at last," the captain said. "What comes of your quest?"

"I found just seven, and nothing compelling."

"...you shall seek all day ere you find them; and, when you have them, they are not worth the search," he recited.

"Yes, it is rather vexing."

He escorted us to a car stop and from there we made our way home. I had little to show for my effort, but by identifying the man with the missing toe I had solved the second mystery and took what satisfaction I could from that.

The newspaper that evening carried a story about the body found in the Gowanus. The man had indeed been murdered—bludgeoned to death, then tossed in the canal. And I had insisted we ignore it! My heart wept. What if that were the murder? What I mean is, the murder that justifies this discursive tale I'm laying before you. You may be thinking, "How could she have been aware there would be a discursive tale to tell which required a murder to justify it while the tale was unfolding?" If pondering that makes your head spin, you know well how I was feeling, for my head was spinning like a top.

IV

For Fanny, other parts of her anatomy were spinning. Half a bottle of brandy on an empty stomach had left her in a delicate state. Michel was ministering to her attentively, but all the while tossing out little bits of sarcasm in his native tongue—all carefully cloaked in solicitous tones. He knew Fanny didn't understand the language well enough to suspect the meaning of the words, and he was foolish enough not to suppose I did. But I said nothing, and gave every indication of being ignorant on the subject. That may sound callous, but one never knows if some future advantage might be gained by familiarity with another's misdeeds. And calling one's mistress "a drunken whore of Babylon" is generally considered adequate grounds for dismissal. If the average student appreciated how useful knowledge of a foreign language can prove, she would show more diligence in the matter. Of course, if we all spoke the foreign tongue equally well, it wouldn't prove nearly so useful—particularly in this case. Rather paradoxical.

Over the next few days, I finished writing the various pieces for our inaugural issue. There was a letter from the publisher, Fanny—written by me, of course. And another from me as editor. Plus two of my adventure stories, the letter from Bangkok, and, at Fanny's insistence, two of her favorite Limericks, with the overly-explicit parts cleverly redacted. It was some days before she allowed me to survey the book, so suspicious was she that I might harm it. It was entitled Cythera's Hymnal, and bore a subtitle I dare not print. It was full of bawdy songs and poetry of a type I wasn't at all familiar with. But Fanny insisted she'd seen much of a similar kind at college. I'd never seen anything of the sort, and told her I found her account doubtful.

"Didn't you ever attend Elizabeth's readings?"

"Elizabeth Strout?"

"Yes, she used to sell tickets for a dollar each. Then she would read a chapter of Justine."

"Justine?"

"The Marquis de Sade. You're so innocent, Emmie."

I'd never thought of myself as innocent, and I disliked intensely being characterized as naïve—especially by someone as simple-minded as Fanny. The more likely explanation for my not being invited to these events was that Elizabeth knew I couldn't spare the price of admission. And if you are wondering, yes, this is the same Elizabeth who may, or may not, have been in Bangkok.

That week Captain Ingalls stopped by twice. The first time was to bring me three conspicuously novel wood-blocks he'd kept for himself. The first showed a skeletal bat-man flying above a city and the second a cow riding on the prow of a locomotive. But the third was the most intriguing. It portrayed a typical scene at the seashore, with a number of fairly ordinary-looking people strolling about, yet the center of attention was a woman of singularly strange construction. She was, in fact, more mollusk than woman. She had the head of a snail, and her derrière had been replaced by its shell. Because she wore the dress of a lady, the rest of her anatomy was difficult to determine. I could tell the captain was much attached to this image, and I promised to return it as soon as I finished printing the first issue. While Fanny entertained our guest, I made some alterations to one of my stories, replacing the Maharini of Valparaíso with the snail-woman of Trieste. It was surprisingly easy.

As you may remember, we had been faced with three mysteries. The first being who was the Marchioness of Karpolov? The second, who was the man with the missing toe? And the third being where was Elizabeth? Having met Captain Ingalls, I had solved the second. That left just one and three, or, if three is now thought to be two with the elimination of the previous number two, one and two.

It was this new juxtaposition of the two remaining mysteries that led me to their common solution, for I at last realized who was behind the appearance of the Marchioness of Karpolov: Madame B_____ herself. I doubted she had played the part, but she had almost certainly orchestrated the bit of theatre. She'd betrayed me. But let me explain the course of my reasoning. You see, she had agreed to allow me to write her biography, provided there was no truth in it. And I had complied faithfully. I'd even sent her drafts, which she told me she'd found very entertaining. Nowhere did I even hint at her current identity. But given her treachery, I may as well reveal all.

The previous summer, Madame B_____ had married a German count and become the Countess von Schnurrenberger und Kesselheim. And not long after that, Elizabeth contrived to become her secretary. (I say contrived because it is generally safe to assume that anything Elizabeth has achieved was gained through contrivance.) The count was posted to the German Embassy in Washington, and the countess—with Elizabeth in tow—joined him there. By coincidence, Harry and I visited that city in December. We met the countess through Elizabeth and saw her on several occasions, twice being invited to the embassy. I soon learned that the countess has a playful nature, and enjoys devising little jests to spring on others. Which brings me to the motivation for her duplicity: the brooch.

The countess had tried to make a fool of me, using an exquisite Lalique brooch as bait. But I had turned the tables and gotten the better of her (and the Lalique). Though she told me I'd been forgiven—and "forgiven" is the word she used—I knew she harbored a lingering resentment. This was made readily apparent when she had her coachman impersonate a policeman and detain us at the train depot, in an effort to reclaim the brooch. He demanded to search our baggage, but found nothing. I had outwitted her again. The Marchioness of Karpolov's threat of a lawsuit was the countess's way of taking revenge.

But who to play the part of marchioness? Who better than Elizabeth—a woman of rare beauty and intelligence, and questionable moral character. And who likewise harbored some lingering—and, I might add, unwarranted—resentment toward me. And so each of the final two mysteries provided the other's solution: Elizabeth had played the part of the Marchioness of Karpolov, ergo, Elizabeth was in New York. Or, put another way, Elizabeth was in New York and the countess needed someone to play the part of the Marchioness of Karpolov, ergo, she persuaded Elizabeth to perform the task. I say persuaded because Elizabeth left her service in December, and not on the best of terms. Of course, one must keep in mind that the countess's usual manner of persuasion very closely resembled what a less single-minded person might term extortion.

The countess had put me in a quandary. If I exposed the Marchioness of Karpolov as a fraud, I exposed my biography of Madame B_____ as a fraud. And so it was that mystery two (or three if you chose not to renumber) was solved, and mystery number one became a conundrum. Though frequently preoccupied with the search for a solution to my dilemma, I returned to work on Psi.

I had just finished the editing when Harry arrived home. And then things became unpleasant rather quickly. Apparently there was nothing in Wilkes-Barre diverting enough to keep his mind off my imagined romance with Michel and so his jealousy had intensified. Then he learned that Michel had been teaching Telemachus to say things like, "Not now, Harry...," as if in imitation of some comment I had made. The next afternoon, when the captain stopped by again, this time making no pretense that his visit was for any reason but to see Fanny, Harry blew up. I had told him that Michel and Fanny were firmly attached to one another, so he had nothing to fear. But seeing the captain there wooing Fanny, he began to suspect I had misled him. When I refused to immediately send Fanny and her servant on their way, Harry grabbed his bag and told me I could find him at his club. He has no club, of course. I assumed he was referring to the Carleton House up in Williamsburg. Harry frequented the saloon there whenever he was in town.

The captain, recognizing the cause of Harry's anger, turned to Michel and advised him, "Come not between the dragon and his wrath."

"Quoi?"

"Just a sound warning, from the good King Lear."

"Quoi?"

"Look out for yourself."

"Quoi?"

In order to put an end to this tedious bit of vaude-ville, I translated for Michel—thus revealing my intimacy with his native language. He realized at once the signifi-cance of my subterfuge: I knew all about the insults he had been casting the way of his employer. He looked at me silently, and swallowed twice. I realized that if I was going to make good use of his compromised state, this was the time to do it. The iron was hot, and I needed to strike.

Fortunately, the stimulatory impetus of necessity acted as muse to my able imagination. I had an idea. I took Michel into the kitchen and recounted some of his choicer abuses of Fanny. He tried to make light of them, but gave up when I reminded him of the epithet "drunk-en whore of Babylon."

Now that I had him cowed, I offered a way out. I would keep quiet about his slurs if he would perform one simple task: attest that he was the Baron Dampierre, the lover of the Marchioness of Karpolov. For once she had been thus exposed, she would have no grounds for a lawsuit regarding her husband. And at the same time, the scandal would generate a good deal of attention in the press for my biography of Madame B_____. It's oft been said that a good scandal is the best publicity. I remember well when the authorities tried to close down Clyde Fitch's Sapho due to its supposed indecency. The ensuing trial turned a mediocre melodrama into a smash hit.

It required most of the afternoon to explain the mat-ter to Michel, but once I had, he agreed. I then tele-phoned Mr. Sackett and asked if he had a way of contacting the marchioness. He told me he had received a note from her saying she would be by the following day at 2 p.m. with a written agreement for him to sign. In it, he was to guarantee he would take no further steps toward publishing my work. I spent the next morning preparing Michel for the great task before him. I had him in one of Harry's best suits, which, to be honest, looked much better on Michel. He really was a handsome man, and had some sense of the deportment of a gentleman. Though I began to suspect he'd never been a valet to any man, especially when he needed my help with the tie.

That's why I was in such an intimate pose with him when Harry walked in. He didn't stay long, but while he was there he made his feelings on the matter very clear. Poor Harry. And, I should add, poor Mary. For the maid still hoped to capture Michel's heart. And now that his employer was regularly entertaining the captain, Michel, a master of deceit, returned Mary's attentions—knowing full well this would arouse Fanny's jealousy. When it did, and this in turn was noticed by the captain, he too became jealous of the Quebecois.

Now, as I'm writing this, the outcome seems painfully obvious. But you must remember that I had been misled by the news of the murdered man found in the Gowanus, and felt no assurance there would be another opportunity for a dramatic climax that would render this a tale worth recording. You, reader, have the advantage of me. I mean me the character, and not me the author. But I think I'm straying a bit.

Michel and I arrived at the office of Baily & Sackett at precisely ten minutes after two. I could hear Mr. Sackett speaking with the marchioness, whose voice I recognized as that of Elizabeth. I gave Michel a signal and he rushed into the room and attempted to embrace the marchioness. I say attempted, because the faux aristocrat responded to his assault by rising from her chair and clubbing him on the side of the head with a paperweight. If I had needed further confirmation that this was Elizabeth, I now had it. She is a stunningly attractive woman, thus well-practiced at discouraging unwanted advances. And both powerful enough and ruthless enough to draw blood.

Michel sat on the floor clutching his cheek and whining in a mixture of French and English that lent a convincing touch to my scheme.

"This, Mr. Sackett, is the Baron Dampierre," I announced. "And I have here his signed affidavit that he has been intimate with the marchioness on thirty-seven occasions in the last six weeks alone."

"Thirty-seven?" he asked.

"Oh, yes. And he is willing to give dates, and details."

"Hello, Emmie."

"Hello, Elizabeth. I thought you were no longer working for the countess."

"I'm not. The dowager asked if I'd like to help her play a little joke on you. She reminded me of the time you blackmailed me into burglarizing that house in Washington and thought I might like an opportunity to get even. And she was right. You remember that night, don't you, Emmie? It was the night I spent in jail."

"Blackmailing you was her idea."

"No doubt. But you were her willing instrument." Then she nodded toward Michel. "Where did you find him?"

"He's Fanny Baum's valet."

"Oh, yes. I've heard of Fanny's valet. What exactly was your plan, Emmie?"

"Well, if I could prove you were the baron's lover, then there would be no basis for your lawsuit alleging that publication of my biography would ruin your marriage to the marquis."

"You mean, your imaginary marquis?"

"Yes, him. I've already arranged to have an account of the affair placed in Town Topics."

"The scandal sheet? I see. But did it occur to you that you might in fact ruin my marriage?"

"Your marriage to the marquis?"

"For god's sake, Emmie. There is no damned marquis! I mean my marriage here in the real world. Do you ever have occasion to visit the real world, Emmie?"

"Oh, that's rich. Coming from the Marchioness of Karpolov. When did you get married?"

"Just before Christmas."

"To that English snob?"

"No, he really did go to Bangkok. But I won't divulge any more. And if you agree not to pry into the matter, I will end my part in this."

"All right, if that's what you want. But it seems rather curious to keep it a secret."

"I have my reasons. Well, I should be on my way."

"Wait, I must know how you managed to have your letter mailed from Bangkok."

"I sent it to the English snob and had him mail it. He was very cooperative—once I'd agreed not to bring a breach of promise suit. Before I go, I will add this. Do not go too far with the countess, Emmie. You no doubt are enjoying your little contests, being just as unbalanced as she is, but you will never match her cold-bloodedness. Remember what happened to the count."

"Oh, I remember." The count had upset the countess—most likely by flirting with Elizabeth—and two days later he choked to death on a chicken bone. You might think it mere coincidence, but this chicken bone had somehow made its way into his Charlotte Russe.

V

Elizabeth gave my cheek a peck and left me there with Mr. Sackett and the wounded baron. If the preceding conversation left you puzzled, imagine its effect on a man of limited intelligence and only a rudimentary understanding of the English language. Michel just sat there on the floor, rubbing his cheek and staring dumbly at whoever was speaking. With his assailant's exit, he pulled himself up and asked if we could leave.

"Just a moment, Baron," Mr. Sackett interjected. "I was wondering if I might have a word."

"Whatever about?" I asked. "We'll hear no more from the marchioness."

"Yes, of course. But that affidavit. And the details of the thirty-seven occasions..."

"Mr. Sackett, what are you suggesting?"

"Well, I know a publisher in Paris. M. Liseux is always looking for interesting material of that nature...."

"A pornographer? We'll have nothing to do with him. Good day, Mr. Sackett. Come along, Michel."

We went back to the apartment and Michel took to his bed. Meanwhile, I began having second thoughts. Perhaps I'd been too hasty with Mr. Sackett. After all, there must be quite a market for books "of that nature." And an aspiring author can't afford to leave any stone unturned, no matter how repugnant she herself finds the stone, or the creatures hiding beneath it. My chief concern was that my knowledge of the subject was too limited in scope. The solution to that was to bring in a collaborator. As it happened, in arranging our subterfuge I had mentioned to Michel the thirty-seven acts, and he had extemporaneously invented an episode that took place on the observation deck of the Eiffel Tower. It was quite convincing, and far too graphic to be incorporated into a serious literary work such as the one before you. We had planned that he would recount the event in Mr. Sackett's office. But Elizabeth's work with the paper-weight had silenced him before he'd a chance to utter a word of it.

Michel had told me earlier he was both willing and able to come up with the other thirty-six episodes. I only wish I had taken him up on this offer immediately. For the very next morning Mary came into my room to tell me Michel appeared to be ill. I followed her into Fanny's room and found him lying on the floor—quite obviously dead. He was on his back, stiff, and with a look of shock on his face.

"Where's Fanny?" I asked.

"I don't know. She wasn't here when I got up. I only came in when I saw the door open, and his arm lying there on the floor."

I made a quick examination of his body and found no wounds, but the thumb and index finger of his right hand were somewhat blackened. As if he had fired a revolver, I thought. I made a search of the room, but found no gun. Or bullet hole. And surely a gun fired so near would have woken Mary and me. This was the fourth and final mystery: Who killed Michel? And quite a good one, I thought. I telephoned the police and about five minutes later a patrolman arrived, and five minutes after that Detective Sergeant O'Brien joined him.

"Looks like an accident," the sergeant pronounced.

"An accident?" I said incredulously. "Look at the expression on his face. It's a look of horror."

"You get that with electrocutions. He must have been plugging in that lamp there. See how the cord is frayed? Just beside the plug. And the black spots on the insulation match the marks on his hand."

"That's very astute, Sergeant."

"Thanks."

"But surely that doesn't mean he wasn't murdered."

"Doesn't it?"

"By no means. What if someone frayed the cord intentionally?"

"What makes you think it was intentional? You know someone who wanted him dead?"

"I can think of several people, each of whom had a clear motive."

"And who might they be?"

There was nothing for it then but to inform the sergeant of all the various jealousies exhibited over the previous days and weeks. Fanny was jealous because Michel seemed to be transferring his attention to Mary. Mary was jealous because she feared he was really faithful to Fanny. Captain Ingalls was jealous because he had seen Fanny jealous. And Harry was jealous because he was a fool. That made four suspects, two motivated by feelings of heated passion turned to hate, and two by just plain hate. Everyone but me had a motive. And, if you're honest about it, dear reader, no one wanted him dead more than you. Weren't you hoping against hope that something—anything—would occur to justify your sticking with this meandering saga? But I suppose it's rather unlikely you were in the vicinity of The Margaret apartments on the night of April 3rd, 1902.

Sergeant O'Brien listened to my account, detailed in every way except in regards to Harry. I'd grown attached to him and wasn't willing to give him up simply on account of his passion for me. But the detective was determined to attribute the death to accidental electrocution.

As it turned out, Fanny had not been home that night, but with the captain. Since she preferred his company, and he had hers, the motives I ascribed to them had evaporated. And since Fanny had abandoned Michel, what motive did Mary have? That left Harry, who I thought had been staying over at the Carleton House in Williamsburg, but in fact had been in Elmira on a new case of fraud. He arrived home just as the sergeant was concluding his investigation.

I imagine you're feeling misled, what with all the suspects being dismissed. But rest assured, it was indeed murder, and the assassin revealed himself just a few days later. That was the afternoon I found Telemachus chewing on an electrical cord in our bedroom. Harry insisted the bird's murder of Michel was a deliberate act. I was willing to entertain that possibility, but then, I asked, who was he trying to do away with in chewing on our cord? Harry didn't have an answer. But the next day he bought a gigantic cage, so Mary wouldn't feel obliged to let the bird fly about the apartment.

In the meantime, the piece I had planted in Town Topics—the society scandal sheet of New York—had done its work. Much interest had been roused by the story of the Marchioness of Karpolov and the Baron Dampierre. I went back to Mr. Sackett's office with the expectation the publicity had made his search for a publisher an easy one.

"Oh, it's out of the question now, I'm afraid," he told me.

"Whatever do you mean? I've seen the references to the marquis and marchioness in all the newspapers."

"That's just it. How long did you think it would be before someone determined there is no Marquis and Marchioness of Karpolov? Or a Baron Dampierre, for that matter. Everyone knows now. And they're making a mockery of it. The World is offering ten thousand dollars to anyone who can prove the existence of the Marquis of Karpolov. And the Journal has a running parody, 'Bellie Nye Scours Europe for Lost Aristocrats.'"

"I've seen that, but surely all publicity is good."

"Not when you're the butt of a joke."

"It's not all fictional. Madame B_____ is real."

"But who will believe that now?"

"What if I were to reveal her true identity?"

"Well, it would be rather easy for her to prove libel, since so much of the story is clearly fabricated. You'd need her consent."

"I'd not be likely to get her consent," I told him. She, no doubt, was relishing my predicament, having been its engineer.

My hopes had been dashed again. But I was not beaten. I spent much of that spring printing the first issue of Psi. The process was absurdly laborious. And filthy. There were ink stains all over the apartment. I quickly decided to reduce the number of pages from thirty-two to sixteen, forcing me to jettison one of my own stories and to condense Fanny's and my letters introducing the magazine into a couple of brief para-graphs. And even still, I only got three dozen copies printed. We made use of most of the wood-blocks, and then Fanny drew by hand an illustration for one of her Limericks. She traced it from a French humor magazine

I'd brought home the year before. I must admit, her renditions came out quite well.

It was mid-June when we hand-delivered the inaugural issue to fellow alumnae living in the city. Twenty-nine altogether, and all twenty-nine subscribed. Even Gloria Bisbee, who was off in Europe, and poor Clara Rockwood, who we belatedly learned had died the year before. Apparently their husbands found my work worthy of further attention, though it might also have had something to do with Fanny's Limericks. It was our inclusion of those poems that necessitated the hand-delivery of the issue, since to mail it would have risked seizure by the postal inspectors.

I was heartened by the positive response, but even allowing for Fanny paying all the expenses the recompense fell well short of my expectations. So I decided there would be no second issue. When I broke the news to Fanny I wasn't at all surprised to find her indifferent. But the more sympathetic captain memorialized the event with a recitation from Much Ado About Nothing:

"Psi no more, ladies, Psi no more,

Men were deceivers ever;

One foot in sea, and one on shore,

To one thing constant never."

His words were more fitting than was at first apparent. Not long after, he withdrew his attentions from Fanny and focused them on Mary. Fanny, having become bored with all things literary, even the Limerick, took it with equanimity. So, with the matter of her male servant resolved, she moved back to her father's palatial Manhattan home. I spent much of the summer printing out copies of a short story I'd written. It was an account of how Harry and I solved the case of a missing shipment of gold on the steamer *L'Aquitaine*, but told from the view-point of the ship's chief rat.

There was an August wedding and once again we were in need of a maid. Neither of us minded, really. It was pleasant to have the apartment to ourselves. Especially with family planning a visit the next month—a visit that would quickly lead us to a new mystery, and a very stimulating adventure.

Ψ

Psi, the Magazine

Please note: Though effort was made to replicate the original magazine as closely as possible, certain compromises were necessary to accommodate an electronic format. If you would like to see the magazine as readers saw it, you may see a surviving copy at:
MeegsMorgue.blogspot.com

Ψ

ΨΨΨΨΨΨΨΨΨΨΨΨΨ

Here's a psi to those who love me,
And a smile to those who hate;
And, whatever sky's above me,
Here's a heart for every fate.

—Lord Byron

PSI

ѱ ѱ ѱ ѱ ѱ ѱ ѱ ѱ ѱ

FRANCINE BAUM, PUBLISHER

EMILY MCGINNIS REESE, EDITOR-IN-CHIEF

ѱ ѱ ѱ ѱ ѱ ѱ ѱ ѱ ѱ

M.E. MEEGS, FICTION EDITOR

ELIZABETH STROUT, BANGKOK CORRESPONDENT

INAUGURAL ISSUE
SPRING, 1902

OFFICES:
34 PLAZA ST.
BROOKLYN, N.Y.

SUBSCRIPTIONS, FIFTY CTS. A YEAR

The story of *Psi* is one of stillbirth and reanimation. And though no demonic arts were employed, or satanic bargains made, its rejuvenation was not without costs, and a good deal of confusion. We are hopeful that you will judge our efforts worthy of your notice and, perchance, patronage.

Ψ Ψ Ψ Ψ Ψ Ψ Ψ Ψ Ψ Ψ Ψ Ψ Ψ

Future issues offer much promise, we believe. Or, put another way, much has been promised for future issues. We can now only hope that Mr. Ibsen follows through with his pledge of a playlet (to be entitled *Naked Under the Northern Lights*), and that the poetic saga Bret Harte had undertaken at our behest was completed before his untimely death earlier this month.

Ψ Ψ Ψ Ψ Ψ Ψ Ψ Ψ Ψ Ψ Ψ Ψ Ψ

...even wise people forget that if a book is worth reading, it is worth buying.

—John Ruskin

THE SNAIL WOMAN OF TRIESTE

I t was a little before midnight, and I was alone in the parlor car of the Serengeti Express, the only direct line between Cairo and the port of Dakar. It was my plan to visit the *maharini* of that city, whom I had met during a sea voyage to Tibet. We had become fast friends during our brief time together and she had insisted I visit her at the familial palace. The train had just left the depot in Constantinople and was crossing the long bridge over the Bosphorus when a woman entered the car. She was dressed all in black, and her face was veiled.

"Forgive me, my dear, for intruding," she said.

"Oh, not at all. I would love some company."

She was older, and spoke with the accent distinctive to the Carpathian Mountains. She sat down in the chair opposite me and promptly pulled a large flask from her bag.

"A small drink, perhaps?"

Not wanting to appear unsociable, I accepted her offer. She filled the empty water glass beside me to the brim. Of course, I recognized the chartreuse libation immediately. We shared a toast, she drinking directly from the flask in large gulps which I would have thought such a frail-looking woman incapable of. As it happens, absinthe is a favorite of mine, and though I usually prefer to have it run over a cube of sugar, I drained my glass of the bitter liquid with equal gusto. She refilled it at once. The steward entered the car and dimmed the lights, in a vain attempt to prompt our retirement. My companion gave him a dismissive wave of her hand.

"Where are you traveling to?" I asked.

"Trieste. I spend every summer at the spa there."

"It sounds lovely."

"And you, my dear? Where might you be going?"

"Dakar, for a brief visit. But after that, nowhere in particular. I have a roving commission from an American newspaper. I stop where I like and then discover some fascinating story for the illustrated magazine they run every Saturday."

"Oh, you would hear many a fascinating story in Trieste."

She then went on to relate one such tale. It involved a woman who suffered horribly from an unnamed affliction. Doctors from across the continent were consulted. They prescribed all sorts of remedies, but none had the least bit of success. Priests came and performed rites, some involving sacrifices. But no good came of it.

"No one could help the snail woman of Trieste. And she was ostracized on account of her great affliction."

"Snail woman, did you say?" I asked.

"Yes, didn't I mention that?"

"Well, you mentioned her incurable affliction."

"No, my dear, you misunderstand. Though she has the body of a snail, she has the soul, and spirit, of a woman. No different from you and me."

"But surely that must pain her, longing for human love, yet unable...."

"Oh, she has many loving friends. And if you mean romantic coupling, she has no need for it."

"Yes, many women take that attitude, but usually only after their hopes have been dashed."

"My dear, her hopes have not been dashed. When I say she has no need for romantic coupling, I'm speaking quite literally. Like many mollusks, she is hermaphroditic. She has dozens of children, but no need for a husband."

"Oh, I see. I suppose there are advantages to that arrangement. Provided one likes children."

"Yes, that is a bit of a problem," she agreed. "It's easy enough to fend off the advances of a husband, but which of us doesn't find herself irresistible?"

We sat silently for a long while, partaking of her flask, and both pondering the truth of her rhetorical question.

"But what then was her affliction?" I asked.

"Well, like yourself she was a writer. And quite successful. She wrote romantic stories based on historical figures."

"Yes, there's quite a lot of that going about these days," I said, perhaps a little too disparagingly. But my companion gave me a look that indicated her agreement with my views on the subject. "So she suffered some illness that kept her from writing?"

"No, she didn't stop writing entirely. It was only the form that changed. She dropped novels and began writing poetry. But on the same themes."

"Oh, dear."

"Yes, they were quite dreadful. And she couldn't stop herself, even for a moment. Couplets before breakfast, then odes until midday, followed by an afternoon of sonnets. Evenings were devoted to ballads, then most of the night to elegies."

"It sounds so frightful."

"It was. But that wasn't the worst of it. She announced that she planned a great epic in verse. Nothing her friends said could dissuade her."

"Hence the doctors?"

"Yes, they tried everything to help her. Cold baths, hot showers, bloodletting, leeches."

"Do mollusks have blood?" I asked, genuinely curious.

"Of a sort. Then the priests were brought in. Catholics, Baptists, Hindus, medicine men. They blessed her, dunked her, levitated her, and finally smoked her out of her own home. But nothing could stop her picking up her pen...."

"What a heartbreaking story. And it is a truly fantastic tale. Unfortunately, my readers have an expectation of fortuitous endings. For instance, if, say, the Hindu cured her and then turned himself into a snail man. Though, in her case, there'd be no advantage in that at all."

"Do all your stories end in the same way?" she asked.

"Oh, no. Certainly not. But if there isn't romantic fulfillment, some sort of grotesquerie is de rigueur. Perhaps if she perished when a street car ran into her and shattered her shell, leaving her an amorphous mass of jelly. Or suppose a mad Frenchman, posing as a doctor and carrying a large supply of garlic and an immense sauté pan...."

"My dear!"

"Oh, do forgive me. I'm afraid the fifth glass of absinthe nearly always leads me astray."

"Well, there is in fact a fortuitous ending to the story. You see, one day a very wise man from Paterson, New Jersey, stopped by the spa and heard the sad story of the snail woman of Trieste. When he learned the nature of her poetry, he asked to see some. Instead of being repulsed, he became overjoyed. He then offered the snail woman a contract for the rights to all her work."

"What on earth did he plan to do with it?"

"He is a music publisher. He said this was just the sort of thing people in America perform in their parlors each evening. Could that be true?"

"Yes, I'm afraid he's right. Not everyone, mind you. But many have gotten rich catering to the taste."

"Then it's no wonder you wander the world, in exile from your home...."

ENTR'ACTE

There was a young lady of Diss

Who went to the river to ****.

> *The man in the [gondola]*

> *Thrust his pole up her ****,*

And gave her most exquisite bliss.

Ed. note: Two words in the above were removed due to their extreme informality, and the term for the type of boat was replaced because the editor feared it would too easily give away the second term mentioned previously. It is a flat-bottomed boat similarly propelled and common on the waterways of England.

LETTER FROM BANGKOK

[We are fortunate in having a correspondent currently residing in Siam. We plan for her informative missives to be a regular feature, providing said correspondent can escape the evil clutches of the chief eunuch, Bukhayt. Ed.]

Dear friend,

So much has transpired since our tearful farewell, I hardly know where to begin. As you remember, I came to this strange city to join my fiancé, Mr. C__, who'd been transferred to the British Embassy here. We had planned that we would marry immediately on my arrival. I had such hopes, such dreams.... Alas! My dreams have turned to nightmares, and my hopes lie trampled in the mud.

Mr. C__ greeted me at the pier with open arms and his usual professions of affection. From there, we went along to a hotel where he had booked me a room, as our nuptials were to take place the next day. The hotel was in a very rundown neighborhood and was itself squalid almost beyond description. Naturally, in traveling to such an exotic locale I had expected privations of various sorts. And I faced them willingly, in the cause of love. This inn, though, was not merely lacking in its amenities. It was a seedy, filthy place, full of dangerous-looking men and aggressive, painted women. The room I was given would rank poor even measured against those of a Bowery flophouse. And decorum prevents my even mentioning the sanitary arrangements.

It was then that Mr. C__, noticing my discomfort, suggested he could arrange for us to be married that very evening. Then we could spend our wedding night in the house he'd already rented. I asked if we couldn't dine first, as I was famished, but he said we must hurry to catch the registrar. We went down to the street and there met a native gentleman whom Mr. C__ introduced as Mr. Kootonga, a friend, he told me. The serendipity of our meeting Mr. Kootonga just as we found ourselves in need of a witness did not escape my notice.

We wound our way through narrow streets and alleys, until we came to a building that looked very similar to the hotel, at least in its decrepitude. There were three or four Chinese gentlemen standing outside, one of whom led us to a small room inside. After a few moments, another Chinese gentleman joined us. He, I was told, would perform the ceremony. It was all in Chinese, so I understood nothing. But at very frequent intervals, both Mr. Kootonga and the registrar would break out in laughter. It was then that I recognized the distinctive odor about the place. Opium. I knew it well from my days working as an investigator for a settlement house.

"Take me away from here!" I demanded of Mr. C__.

"Whatever is the matter, my dear?" he asked.

"I insist you take me to a proper hotel, at once."

"But my dear, we're man and wife now."

He looked to the registrar, who nodded agreement—all the while grinning like an idiot.

"I've had enough of this farce. If you won't take me to a hotel, then take me to the American Embassy."

"It's unfortunate you've become so unreasonable, my dear. I had hoped to enjoy our wedding night before we needed to part."

"Needed to part? What are you talking about?"

He didn't answer, but turned to Mr. Kootonga. They conversed in the native tongue and then Mr. Kootonga handed him a small pouch.

"Good-bye, my dear."

And that was the last I saw of Mr. C__. The so-called registrar then grabbed me and held me tightly while Mr. Kootonga bound and gagged me. Then they carried me out and tossed me into a wagon of rotting vegetables and covered me with a tarp. We traveled for what seemed like hours, over rutted streets and through a cacophony of sounds.

When we at last arrived at our destination, I was carried off the cart and up some stairs. We entered a large stone building of unusual design. Doors were opened and closed as we went from room to room until finally I was tossed to the floor. Another man entered the room and spoke with Mr. Kootonga. I was unbound, but not to be given my freedom, only to make it easier for them to increase my degradation by stripping me naked! Oh, a sad day....

Still gagged, and my wrists held tightly, I was poked, and patted, like a chicken at market. The man inspecting me was of immense physique, dressed in colorful silks and with a scimitar hanging from the sash that girded him. Then my gag was removed. I made to scream out,

 but with powerful hands he held my jaw open wide, then peered in, as if trying to judge the age of a nag. And if that weren't enough, he went on to carefully examine each of my other orific-es—as if expecting to find some hidden treasure.

When he completed his tour, he handed Mr. Kootonga a purse, easily triple the size of that which Mr. C__ had received. Though my soul was in anguish, I took some satisfaction in the fact my betrayer had made such a poor bargain. Then Mr. Kootonga and his companion left me with the silk-robed giant. He went to the door and clapped his hands loudly. In an instant, a half dozen young women came into the room. He gave them instruc-tions and left as they bowed in obedience.

For the first time since my arrival in this strange land, I was treated with gentleness. They petted me, and cooed sympathetically, then led me to a room with a large marble pool. First, they carefully washed off the filth and repugnant odors I'd accumulated during my travails, and only then brought me to the warm, per-fumed waters of the pool. No bath has ever provided as much comfort as that. They let me bask in it as long as I wished, then dried me, and finally dressed me in clothes like their own—undergarments of the softest silk one can imagine, and a loose-fitting blouse and matching, billowing trousers.

Then they led me to a large room filled with couches and pillows, and a good many more similarly clad women. At the doorways large, silent men stood sentinel. We sat down and shared a sumptuous feast, the like of which I'd never experienced. All sorts of pastries, some sweet, some filled with spiced meat, eggs of some unknown species, and fruits of odd, suggestive shapes.

All of my companions spoke in languages I did not recognize. And though they came in many races, several looked of European ancestry. I tried speaking to them in French, German and Italian. They didn't understand—even when I tried Latin and Greek. Then, at last, a beautiful young woman with flowing black hair and an ivory complexion entered the room. She approached me and, to my relief, spoke to me in English, of the Irish variety.

When I told her my woeful tale, she smiled.

"Oh, you must have been sold to Bukhayt, the chief eunuch. I wonder what he paid for you?"

"Yes, an interesting question. But setting aside the pecuniary considerations, how do I find my way out of here?"

"I don't think anyone ever has."

"Were you brought here under similar circumstances?" I asked her.

"No, not very similar."

She told me a most fantastic tale. She'd come to the East with missionaries but became separated from her group as they passed through the Khyber Pass and found herself the captive of a native chieftain. From there, she changed hands several times, until eventually landing in her current domicile.

"But where are we, exactly?" I asked.

"Don't you know? We are the harem of the Great King of the White Elephant."

She said this as if she were quite proud of the achievement.

"You mean, this king has his way with each and every one of you?"

"Well, just as many of us have our way with him. He's actually quite young, and the handsomest man I've ever met."

"But don't you long for your freedom? To return to the work of a missionary?"

"Oh god, no. Do you know what it's like living with those people? And the food...."

"But why did you sign on with them in the first place?"

"To get out of Limerick, of course. I always planned to abandon the work when we reached the East. That kidnapping was the best thing that ever happened to me."

I was not of the same mind as my new friend. But later that night, when I was summoned to the King's chamber, I found she had not exaggerated his exquisite beauty. He told me he found me irresistible, but I imagine it was my novelty that attracted him most. It would have been quite easy for me to succumb to his charms, but I was determined to escape with my virtue more or less intact. A diversion was necessary, and the only one that came to mind was that tired old chestnut women in harems had been using since time immemorial: I would do as Scheherazade.

I used as my text the *Metamorphoses* of Apuleius, or at least the bits of it I remembered. Only I bent the tale to fit my needs. In my version Fotis holds her virginity more dear, and it is in order to fend off the advances of her aggressive suitor that she changes him into a donkey. I implied I was privy to the secrets of her sorcery, hoping this would instill a certain caution in my own would-be lover. I continued the tales for six nights running, but I knew the King was losing patience. He pointed out that the fifth tale was nearly identical to the second, and the sixth made no sense at all. The next night, he told me, he'd have me gagged! I was filled with worry the following morning. I knew that I must either escape the palace—or become expert at pantomime—by nightfall. What was I to do?

To be continued...

ENVOI

A young woman got married at Chester,
Her mother she kissed and she blessed her.
*   Says she, "You're in luck,*
*   He's a stunning good [fellow],*
For I've [met] him myself down in Leices-
ter."

Ed. note: Certain obscure words of Saxon origin were
improved upon for the sake of clarity.

Babes at Sea

by

M.E. Meegs

A short glossary has been provided at the end of the novella, on page 254.

1

The muffled clatter of rain on slate infused the grubby attic room of the grubby inn with a palpable gloom, while the relentless drip caught by a cracked chamber pot provided an unnecessary reminder of the wretchedness of her state... *plic... plic... plic....*

For five days, Mrs. Biddle had waited for word. For five days, tension waxed as food and money waned—just as it had throughout the long, wet French spring... *plic... plic... plic....*

Eight months on the Pas-de-Calais, the last three in another leaking attic room, where for the first time in her life Mrs. Biddle had been compelled to accept charity. And that she resented most of all. Resented the fact of it, if not the cause. Now, in this last week of May, she had come to Cherbourg on a vague promise from a dubious man. And for five days and nights, she waited... *plic... plic... plic....*

Her mood, never one that could be judged sunny, had turned as foul as the weather. Still, as she sponged herself before the few remaining shards of a shattered mirror, Mrs. Biddle took solace in the resplendent, if intermittent, view. She had recovered nicely from her long infirmity. And what was privation to a woman who fed on adversity as lesser women feed on pastry? Tension for her was simply the unavoidable precursor to action. In this she resembled nothing so much as a coiled spring. A rather good-looking coiled spring, to be sure. Few others sported so statuesque a figure, so clear a complexion, or so blonde and lush a mane. As frequently happened, Mrs. Biddle was cheered by her own superiority. But, speaking honestly, she couldn't deny she was a coiled spring in dire need of a good bath.

She had just finished dressing when there was a knock.

"*Un message, madame.*"

Mrs. Biddle opened the door and took a handwritten note from a boy in an ill-fitting uniform. As she read, he waited. She looked down at him in disgust.

"*Va-t'en!*" she shouted.

He made a face, then spat back over his shoulder, "*Gadoue!*"

It was with the slamming of the door that the fruit of Mrs. Biddle's recent infirmity announced herself from her makeshift cradle—a small drawer suspended by cord from the peak of a dormer. Her mother picked her up and brought her to the bed. Then hoped against hope that the well had not yet run dry. For like her mother, Eugenia was not one to give up easily.

The name—meaning as it does *well-born*—was chosen as testament to Mrs. Biddle's own opinion of herself. How could her daughter be otherwise? She did, of course, resent the encumbrance on a life which had been kept scrupulously free of encumbrances. Not even marriage was allowed to impinge upon Mrs. Biddle's devotion to self. But here, at her breast, was an extension of that self, and even if she loved the child only half so much as she loved herself—a daughter's chromosomal entitlement—it would still be far more than any self-abnegating genetrix could muster.

"*Bonjour*, little sister!"

A petite girl—no older than seventeen, but last

called ingénue at twelve—entered the room bearing a baguette and two pots. She set these on the table, then pulled an orange from one pocket of her jacket and a parcel of soft cheese from the other.

"Where did you spend the night?" Mrs. Biddle asked bitterly.

"Making sure baby sister has some breakfast beside the milk of a witch," the girl answered in a thick French accent, but nearly correct grammar.

After throwing off her jacket, she tied her russet hair into a loose knot, then pried the baby from her mother— the latter making no protest. She sat down at the table and dunked a finger in the pot of milky chocolate, then let the baby curled in her arm suckle it. Mrs. Biddle rose and rebuttoned her blouse before the broken mirror.

"This is for you to eat," the girl said, nodding toward the food but not looking upon the woman at the mirror. "I've well eaten."

"Your belly full, is it? Have a care, girl, or soon you'll find yourself with your own little sister. Or the pox."

"That makes nothing to me," the girl told her as she waved the small bottle of holy water she wore on a string about her neck and depended on as spiritual prophylactic.

"Simple peasant. You think that protection enough when you spend the night passing yourself about?"

"I *do not* pass myself about!" the girl shouted back indignantly. Realizing her tone had unsettled Eugenia, she softened it. "I was with a... *éminent* man, the husband of the mistress of the mayor."

"He told you the mayor beds his wife?"

"Yes. And why not? It is a... *honneur?*"

"Honor. So, I have the mayor's cuckold to thank for

my breakfast?" Her pride temporarily subdued by the aroma of cheese and coffee, Mrs. Biddle took a place at the table.

"No. This is for baby sister—you are the cow it must go through first."

"Then I suppose I must eat my grass."

"And say *meuh!*" the girl added for the benefit of her little sister.

"I'm an American cow," Mrs. Biddle corrected. Then, in a display that would have shocked any who knew her in the prenatal past, she gave her child a spirited "*moo-oo!*"

"So the cows talk different also?" the girl asked.

"Yes, and the roosters."

"No *cocorico?*"

"*Cockadoodledoo!*"

While her elders went through their bilingual bestiary, Eugenia, quite reasonably, looked on in stupefaction. Barely three weeks out of the womb, she had not yet learned an infant must pay for her keep by lavishing signs of amusement on her caretakers whenever they chose to degrade themselves. She *was* grateful for the chocolate her benefactress had provided, but surely she had adequately expressed her appreciation by not immediately regurgitating it upon the girl's blouse.

In truth, the girl—Mélisande, she called herself—was not even ten years younger than her "little sister's" mother. Though her exact role was a matter of continuous debate, she was an adjunct acquired during the previous winter. She had arrived in Étaples sometime before Christmas and Mrs. Biddle had made occasional use of her as factotum, with the girl wanting no payment beyond lessons in English. It was, she claimed, with that objective that she had come to the colony of Anglophones on the Pas-de-Calais.

When the money ran low and Mrs. Biddle economized by moving to the hostel's attic, the artful girl attended her more frequently—like the others at Étaples, she was convinced that sooner or later the proud woman would wire home for passage. For her own part, Mrs. Biddle knew full well the girl was merely ingratiating herself in the hope of securing a berth on the inevitable return voyage to New York. And Mélisande knew that Mrs. Biddle knew.

When spring arrived and the pregnancy proved difficult, Mélisande took on the duties of nurse, and her self-serving motives were mildly diluted with something resembling compassion. But the birth of Eugenia changed everything. Mrs. Biddle was completely dependent on the girl for two weeks, by the end of which Mélisande's devotion to her "little sister" had become fact.

As a nearby bell struck one, the insufferably precious game ended when neither patron nor retainer could remember the call of a rhinoceros. Her dignified demeanor restored, Mrs. Biddle rose from the table and announced they would be sailing that evening.

Mélisande was ecstatic. Six months of attending this contumelious shrew had worn thin even her good humor. Now, at last, she was sailing to New York. And not as an ignorant provincial likely to end up the exotic in some tenderloin house of sport. She had used her time in Étaples wisely, mingling freely with the expatriate poets and artists—in some cases quite freely—and would arrive in New York thoroughly fly.

"I must go off to make arrangements," Mrs. Biddle

told her. "You'll need to start packing. We catch a boat from the Gare Maritime at five."

On picking up her jacket, Mrs. Biddle displaced that of the girl. The gold fob of a watch peeked out from a pocket. With a subtle grace born of careful breeding, Mrs. Biddle palmed the watch and slid it into her bag.

Down below, she negotiated her way through the damp, narrow lane, past the broken glass, half-eaten fruit, and filthy progeny of the slum, trying in vain to ignore the over-powering stench of urine. When an inebriated sailor slouching in a doorway made a suggestion she thought demeaning, Mrs. Biddle spat on him without turning her head. Though few would guess it to look at her—especially those unacquainted with her expectorial marksmanship—Mrs. Biddle was no stranger to her milieu. Her first memories were of a street indistinguishable from this in all its essentials, if not its particulars. The drunken sailor, for instance, who now stumbled from his haunt and challenged her with insulting gibes, would have been wearing the uniform of the U.S. Navy rather than that of the French. But if the menace was universal, the methodology employed in confronting it was quite personal. Mrs. Biddle lowered her arm and shook her sleeve. A straight razor fell into her palm.

Today, however, there would be no need for threatening gestures. Just ahead a sergeant of police turned onto the block, followed by two gendarmes. As they passed, Mrs. Biddle acknowledged the sergeant's suggestive smile with a stern look of reproach. When the sailor made a complaint against her, the already annoyed policeman shoved him to the street without slackening his pace.

II

Ten minutes later, Mrs. Biddle was in the lobby of the Hôtel de l'Aigle. But it was five minutes more before the other made his appearance. She knew that no matter what time she arrived, he would materialize some minutes later. He was a man of petty habits. The type of man who would hide himself in a corner of a hotel lobby behind a newspaper he couldn't read.

"I'm sorry I'm late, my dear," the man currently calling himself Dowling proffered.

Mrs. Biddle said nothing, simply smiled contemptuously at the copy of *Le Figaro* he'd placed on a table. There was no need for her to embarrass him further by inquiring in her perfect French what he'd gleaned from his reading. He averted his gaze, needlessly patting his thin grey hair. Mrs. Biddle had drawn first blood.

"Why no word for five days?" she demanded.

"There was no word to send, my dear. When he didn't board the *Deutschland*, it became a game of wait and see. It was only this morning I heard he'd be sailing on the *Kronprinz Wilhelm*. They should have left Southampton an hour ago."

"And who is 'he'?"

"'He' is the perfect dupe, a jay-town rube as wealthy as Midas. Name's Dexter. Timothy Dexter. He's on his way home. With Archie Cobb as his valet. Do you remember Archie?"

"A bald Englishman? Favored the drop game?"

"Yes, but he has other talents," Dowling assured her.

"And he's the one who spotted this Dexter?"

"That was another Englishman, a friend of Archie's. This fellow had some elaborate game going that went off the track. When it was over, all he had to show for it was the rusting hulk of a steamer stuck in the mud near the mouth of the Thames. Not only was it worthless, he'd been enjoined to have it towed off. Well, he meets this Dexter while loitering about the Métropole, sees he's an easy mark, and by the next morning he's sold him the wreck for ten thousand dollars, *cash*."

"How much more does he have?"

"From what he's heard, Archie thinks there must be fifty thousand more."

"And my share?"

"A full twenty percent."

"And you and Cobb? Forty each?"

"He's put a lot of work into this, and I've put up quite a bit of capital. Securing cabins at the last minute doesn't come cheap. It's only fair."

"Twenty-five."

"Well, it will have to come from mine... but I guess I can't deny you that," Dowling acquiesced, then added with affected beneficence, "I always was soft on you."

A slight, upward curl appeared on Mrs. Biddle's upper lip. Those of her acquaintances familiar with it took it as a signal to seek safer quarters. Dowling examined the crease of his trousers.

But Mrs. Biddle knew she had lost the round. His ready compliance meant that he'd probably offered Cobb a twenty percent share, saying *she* was getting forty. Then agreed to raise Cobb's portion to twenty-five out of feigned friendship. Now the old man would be taking a full half for himself. It wasn't the first time she had allowed him to cheat her. But she swore it would be the last.

"Just what do you have in mind?" she asked.

"We sell him the deed to an underwater duchy."

"An underwater duchy?"

"Yes. You see, there's a fictional syndicate with plans to build a railway tunnel under the channel, Dover to Calais. And you are the heiress of a duchy that became submerged about the time of the Norman Conquest. The syndicate needs the deed to complete the tunnel."

"Are you serious?"

"Perfectly. I grant it's a little baroque, but that's what you need for a fellow like this. I'll be posing as agent for the syndicate, following you across to get the deed. Archie convinces Dexter he can clean up by getting in front of me, then selling it to the syndicate for a healthy profit."

"What deed?"

"Well, grant, more properly."

He produced an antiqued document written in monastic calligraphy on brittle parchment. Writ large across the top were the two words *Ducatus Aquatiquus*, and affixed at the bottom was the wax seal of Charlemagne—conveniently rendered in modern nomenclature. The text between began, "*Osculetur me osculo oris sui*," which Mrs. Biddle recognized as the offering of a kiss that opens the Song of Solomon. On the reverse was a crude map demarcating the borders of the duchy—a geographic pustule rising from the epidermis of northern France.

"You are Lady Eleanor Marsouin of Aquatique," Dowling went on. "Traveling incognito, of course, posing as an American, Elsbeth Duncan. That way, if your accent fails you, there's a ready excuse. Though I doubt Dexter would notice one way or the other."

Mrs. Biddle bristled at the suggestion any aspect of her being could fail her.

"I'll need two hundred francs and the same amount in dollars," she told him. However dubious the scheme, if it got her to New York with even a modest amount of cash, she would be content.

"What for? Your cabin's paid for, *with a bath*. Do you have any idea what that costs?"

Mrs. Biddle said nothing, simply sat stone-faced until the other took out his wallet and placed two hundred francs on the table.

"That's all I have with me," he told her. In fact, he could easily have produced the two hundred dollars. But he had no intention of insulating her from failure. "One other thing, my dear. I've arranged to have a woman travel as your maid. There's plenty of room in your cabin, and it will lend credibility to your story."

"Who?"

"Her name's Céleste. She's top-notch, helped me through a difficult night in Trouville."

Mrs. Biddle smiled at his revelation. "I have my own maid," she told him. "Your paramour can travel in your own cabin."

"Leave yours behind. Or send her steerage," the old man told her. "I'm sorry, my dear, but on this I must insist."

Sensing Dowling's resolve could more easily be circumvented than assaulted frontally, Mrs. Biddle silently gathered the banknotes from the table and placed them in her bag.

"So I'll see you at five o'clock?" the other asked. On Mrs. Biddle's nod, he added, "Céleste will be on the tender but standing apart. She'll approach you."

Outside, Mrs. Biddle for the first time connected the sergeant of police with the watch she'd taken from Mélisande's jacket. She took it out and read the inscription carved on the case, *À M. Bouc, de son cher ami M. Cocu-fieur, le maire de Cherbourg*. Many were the ways of the French that irritated Mrs. Biddle, but she felt obliged to admire the frankness with which they approached matters of the heart. It was difficult to imagine an American cuckold accepting a commemorative gold watch from his wife's lover.

Eugenia! Mrs. Biddle, still unaccustomed to troubling herself over another being, picked up her pace. At the inn's street door, a gendarme stood chatting with a working girl. Mrs. Biddle passed them and upstairs encountered the second gendarme with his ear to the door of her room. He made a feeble attempt to stop her, but she pushed him aside.

The queer scene that greeted her prompted a strange sense of relief. Eugenia was flying about the room in the hands of a prancing police sergeant, naked from the waist down, while Mélisande watched bare-breasted from the bed, shrieking encouragement. At the sound of the door the sergeant instinctively covered his modesty with the only shield at hand. Mrs. Biddle took her child from him, and while he hurriedly dressed, spoke to him in French.

"You came for the watch of Monsieur Bouc?"

"Yes, madame. But...," he nodded toward Mélisande.

"Yes, I see you've been paid. But it would be to your advantage to have the watch as well, *n'est-ce pas?*"

"You have it, madame?"

"Be at the Gare Maritime at five o'clock this afternoon, where the boat for the Lloyd line docks. You will see a woman approach me. Wait until I nod—she will have the watch. You may not be able to charge her, but hold her until the boat departs."

"As you say, madame." He gave her a short bow and made his exit.

Mélisande, shameless as always, sang a vulgar ditty while she dressed.

"You took my watch, madame. It was a gift."

"Why must you always lie to me?" Mrs. Biddle asked. "You lie with a cuckold and steal his watch. Then you need to lie with the... *flique*. You need to give up the thieving and whoring if you want to come with me to New York."

"And the lying?"

"Yes, and the lying."

"Which lying? There *seems* to be two. One is a sin. The other a... *occase?*"

"Opportunity? What are you talking about?"

"Well, if I go to confession and I tell the priest, 'Father, I have sinned. I lied *to* my father,' he will tell me I must say thirty Ave Marias. But if the next week I say, 'Father, I have sinned. I lied *with* my uncle for a...' *franc?*"

"Two bits."

"'I lied *with* my uncle for two bits,' the holy father will tell me how I can make three bits without leaving the confessional."

"You wicked girl." Try as she might, Mrs. Biddle was unable to suppress a smile. "But you *lay* with your uncle—and you can't have three bits."

"Why can't I?"

"Bits only come in twos. So, two bits, or four bits, but not one bit, or three bits."

"That is very silly."

"Yes, best to stick with dollars and cents. Now we need to hurry and pack."

The coiled spring had sprung....

2

While Mrs. Biddle prepared her party for its evening departure aboard the S.S. *Kronprinz Wilhelm*, Tomasz Szczęsny—a distracted young man who spent a good part of his day trying to keep his tie straight, hair combed, and shirt tucked in—was leaving that ship's telegraph office with a cable for his employer.

It took very little to distract Tomasz. The weather alone—be it sunny or dreary, arid or damp—often led his thoughts astray. Place him on a bustling London thoroughfare, or even a moderately busy street in his native Łodz, and he would, within seconds, be lost in contemplation of the countless human dramas playing out before him. On one memorable autumn afternoon, the sight of a forlorn-looking rat traversing an alley sent him into an hours-long reverie that was broken only when a resident some floors above thought it an opportune moment for emptying her chamber pot.

The sad truth was, Tomasz Szczęsny had the heart of a poet. Worse still, he had the mind of a poet. But, at least in the eyes of his friends, he did have one saving grace: he did not write poetry.

Tomasz had no time for writing poetry. His domineering father had instilled in him a sense of familial duty that precluded such frivolous pursuits. For it would be up to this unassuming boy to regain some semblance of his family's former prestige. The Szczęsnys, you see, had been of the minor nobility until dispossessed during one of the eighteenth-century partitions of Poland.

Tomasz was never quite sure which of the several partitions it was, or whether the family estate was lost to the Prussians or the Austrians, only that it was up to him, and him alone, to remedy the situation as best he could.

As the Polish kingdom had been dismembered into oblivion, and the doling out of aristocratic titles therefore in abeyance, it would be necessary to venture further afield. Tomasz's father set his sights on Victoria's England—seat of a sprawling empire of unimaginable wealth, and one which had demonstrated its good breeding by having never invaded Poland. He sent his son to the University of Krakow, where he could learn a passable English at modest expense, and, more recently, financed his trip to London. The goal: to marry the daughter of a duke, a marquess, or, if absolutely unavoidable, an earl. But nothing less would do, for she must bear the title of Lady. His father made it quite clear that if he returned home the son-in-law of a mere baronet, he could expect disinheritance. Rather an empty threat, as there was not much left worth inheriting. But so thoroughly had his father conditioned Tomasz that he went to England with the sincere intention of carrying out his sire's desire.

Regrettably, Tomasz arrived in England just as the vogue for marrying aristocratic issue to American millionaires was hitting its stride. What the average duke was looking for in a son-in-law was a man who could shore up the family finances with ample sums of a sound currency. Fanciful Poles residing in third-rate Chelsea boarding houses were not high on his list.

It was just after breakfast one morning at his third-rate boarding house that Tomasz was presented with what seemed a simple solution: *become* an American millionaire. He was speaking with another inmate of the house, a man named Archie Cobb, who some days earlier had been told of Tomasz's predicament. Archie informed him that he had recently taken the position of gentleman's gentleman to a wealthy American and that he had been tasked with finding a secretary to serve the same master.

"Just think of it, Tommy," Archie enthused. "You'll be privy to all the secrets of the trade. See it as an apprenticeship. In a year or two you go off on your own, make your own fortune, and quicker 'an you can say Jack Robinson, you'll have to beat back those blue bloods with a club. Why, every evening your mail will be flooded with invitations to house parties, theatre outings, fancy-dress balls. All the best hunts will be badgering you to sign on. This is an opportunity you can't afford to pass up, my boy. You know what they say—when fortune smiles, embrace her. Then take her off to a quiet corner, that's what I say."

While it did seem odd that a man who made his living performing tricks for the theatre crowds of Covent Garden was in a position to mete out appointments to the entourage of an American millionaire, Tomasz suppressed his skepticism and allowed his inner poet to lay out a convincing case that led to his acceptance of the adventuresome plan. And so it was that only a few hours before our meeting him, Tomasz had boarded the *Kronprinz Wilhelm* as secretary to Timothy Dexter.

You will, dear reader, find it illustrative of how easily Tomasz could be distracted when I reveal that during my long explication of his circumstances, he'd gotten no further than the promenade deck, just one deck below that of the telegraph office. While descending the stairs, he had caught sight of a charming young woman looking back over her shoulder. Not at him, but in his general direction. That was all it took.

Tomasz wandered after her, soon losing her in the crowd. Then, a moment later, she emerged, now walking toward him. She was herself distracted, reading a letter as she hastened along. He could see at once that she was a woman of passion, the way her lips quivered as she read, the way her eyes seemed to feed on the words, the way she blushed at one particular passage. A man called her from behind, and as she turned to look, she collided with Tomasz.

"Take this for me and destroy it," she said, pushing the letter into Tomasz's hand. She was German, scented with lavender. "Go. Quickly!"

Never one to fail a lady in distress, Tomasz took her offering and hurried below. When he reached the upper cabin deck, he paused to peruse the letter. It was a billet-doux. And a particularly piquant one, at that. He was glad now that he had spent so much time at university learning the idiomatic vocabulary of the female anatomy in each of the languages he was assigned to master, as the vibrant argot used in the penultimate paragraph bore a striking resemblance to that of a pornographic novella his German roommate had shared with him. It would be a crime to destroy so artistic a missive. Someday, Tomasz felt sure, he would need to come up with just this sort of communiqué. He put it in his pocket, pushed his unruly black hair out of his eyes, and knocked on the door of his employer's cabin.

"You may come forth," Timothy Dexter called from within.

"I have the cable, sir," Tomasz informed him, tucking in his shirt tail as he did so.

"Read it, boy. Read it."

"Sir, we have received what we believe a very generous offer of six hundred pounds for the S.S. *Oblinibat* from a reputable scrap dealer, buyer to bear all costs. Please send instructions. Signed, Nye, Clare & Co."

"Six hundred pounds, sterling! That's three thousand dollars, boy. A comely, buxom profit." As he so often was, Timothy Dexter was excited. And when Timothy Dexter became excited, his snow-white eyebrows hopped about his forehead like a pair of rabbits performing a synchronized ballet.

"Is this the steamship that is broken in the Thames?"

"One and the same. I had a feeling it would be worth something as scrap. Price of iron was due for a rise."

"How could you be sure?" Tomasz asked, hoping to glean his first piece of financial acumen.

"Never sure, boy. Never sure. Just felt it. Then I meet a fellow without leaving my hotel willing to sell the title to five thousand tons of iron, and I know the gods want me to buy." The right eyebrow did a solo pirouette.

"For how much did you buy it?"

"A mere ten thousand."

"Ten thousand dollars?"

"Yes, ten thousand of the genuine article."

This confused Tomasz a good deal. He freely admitted the market economy was a closed book to him. Still, how could selling for three thousand dollars what you bought for ten thousand be profitable? It would, he feared, be a long apprenticeship....

"Shall I take a letter in reply?" Tomasz asked. "I should be able to mail it when we reach Cherbourg."

"Good thinking, boy. Yes, take a letter." Dexter

rummaged through one of the several stacks of paper lying on the floor until he found one with the address of the firm. "To Nye, Clare & Co., 88, Bishops Gate Within," he read, then stopped. "Within what?" he asked.

"Perhaps it means they have offices at that address, but no sign outside," Tomasz suggested.

"Very shrewd, boy, very shrewd. Well, let's get back to it. Sirs, have received your cable and answer it with esteemed affirmation."

"Does that mean they should sell it?" Tomasz asked.

"Yes, sell the damn thing, and send payment to my solicitors." There was another pause while Dexter again searched his piles of papers.

"Perhaps it would be helpful if I were to organize your correspondence?"

"Let *you* have my papers? Never, boy. Never. Ah, here it is. Send payment to my solicitors, Crowders, Vizard, Oldham & Co., 51, Lincoln's Inn Fields. Yours benevolently, Timothy Dexter."

"I will type this immediately, sir, and bring it back for your signature."

"Sound plan, boy. And send Archie around."

Tomasz made a slight bow and went off to the cabin he shared with Archie Cobb, thus interrupting what had been a very thorough—and thoroughly fruitless—search of his belongings.

"How's the old man?" Cobb asked.

"Oh, very happy. Though I don't understand it. You know that steamship he bought?"

"The one stuck in the mud?" Cobb smiled.

"Yes. He's sold it for three thousand dollars and says it is a nice profit. How can that be when he paid ten thousand of the genuine article for it?"

"Did he use the term 'genuine article'?" Archie Cobb swallowed hard.

"Yes. Is that better than banknotes?"

"It depends which side of the transaction you're on." A note of despondency colored Archie's voice. In his circles, the term "genuine article" was used only ironically, to refer to currency of private manufacture. Had his old friend Len Bailey sold his steamship for a pile of counterfeit bills? Seemed impossible. No, more likely Dexter had used the term not knowing its meaning to the cognoscenti.

"There can't have been a profit," Archie insisted. "He's mad. Knew it from the moment I laid eyes on him. From what I've heard, all these American millionaires are as mad as hatters. We just have to humor him. If he says he made a profit, there's nothing for it but to congratulate him."

"I see," Tomasz said. But something new troubled him. "Do you think it will be necessary for me to go mad if I'm to be a millionaire?"

"As sure as eggs is eggs, but what will it matter? You'll always have people about telling you what a genius you are, at least as long as the money holds out."

"And the blue bloods? They won't mind me marrying one of their daughters?"

"Them? They're even battier—all that inbreeding."

"Ah," Tomasz said, relieved. He took out his Blickenderfer Model 7, the odd-looking typewriter his new employer had provided, and placed it on the tiny table. "Oh, by the way. The old man wants to see you."

"All right. I don't suppose he's given you a key to his cabin?"

"Key? No, he won't even trust me with his papers.

How can I be his secretary if I can't see his papers?"

"Just remember, he's rich, and we're not."

II

Archie Cobb was a man of vague middle age, forty-five at least, but not yet sixty, by no means svelte, but not particularly fat, with a bald, round pate that led directly to an equally round forehead. The latter of which was currently covered in a thin layer of moisture born of concern. Moments earlier he had quelled his anxiety over the authenticity of Dexter's store of cash, but dark doubts now clouded his conviction.

For himself, he didn't mind in the least being employed by a man who made his fortune passing the queer. What did worry him was the reaction of his accomplice, Dowling. Though generally not violent, Dowling was known to be vindictive—perhaps the most vindictive man in Archie's exceptionally wide acquaintance. It was imperative that he determine the character of Dexter's currency at the earliest possible moment. Then, if it proved only ironically genuine, Archie could disembark at Cherbourg—with luck, unseen by Dowling.

Timothy Dexter answered his knock with his customary, "You may come forth."

"I understand you have need for me, sir," Archie said, then began straightening things about the cabin. When he opened the wardrobe, Dexter took hold of his shoulder and spun him around.

"What are you doing?" he demanded.

"Seeing to your apparel, sir. It *is* one of the chief concerns of a valet."

"Never mind that. You only have to play the valet

until we reach New York. After that I have something else I need you to do. You ever do any acting?"

"Oh, yes, sir. I feel, sometimes, that my life has been one long performance."

"Good. Then this should be easy for you. I need you to play an English lord."

"Of any particular station?"

"Station?"

"I mean, shall I be a duke? An earl?"

"Doesn't matter, just so people have to call you Lord."

"Then I suggest a viscount—more difficult to check up on. The Viscount of Abernethy. My mother's people are from Abernethy. For whose benefit will I be performing this role?"

"It's to satisfy my wife. I told her I'd bring back a lord for our daughter to marry. But the real ones ran too dear. I can't see spending good money to buy myself a son-in-law that's more tapeworm than man."

"I see. You wish me to marry your daughter." Archie had seen a photograph of Felicia Dexter, and though the prospect of matrimony had never before appealed, he was more than willing to explore the subject with the curvaceous young lady in question. "You are wise to close the matter forthwith. Daughters and dead fish are no keeping wares."

"Hell, she hasn't gone off yet. No, I don't want you to marry my daughter, just satisfy my wife. One look at you and the girl will have nothing to do with you. No offense."

"None taken. And once I've satisfied Mrs. Dexter, what becomes of me then?"

"We'll have to see about that, later."

It sounded decidedly indefinite. Archie preferred the

security of hard cash. It was time to lay the groundwork for Dowling's scheme.

"Speaking of the aristocracy, I have heard, sir, that Lady Eleanor Marsouin of the lost Duchy of Aquatique will be boarding in Cherbourg."

"How'd she lose her duchy? Cards or dice?"

"The duchy was lost to the waters of time, submerged in a great earthquake some centuries back."

"Can't have much of an income from that."

"No, sir. Quite true. But the duchy is now sought after by the syndicate building the cross-channel tunnel."

"What tunnel?" Dexter asked.

"The rail tunnel which will proceed under the channel from Dover to Calais. Surely you've read about it in the financial press."

"What use have I for the financial press?"

His attitude came as a relief to Archie, but did not surprise him. Whatever means Dexter had used to acquire his fortune, there was no doubt they were of an unorthodox nature.

"It appears," Archie explained, "the drowned duchy lies in the path of the tunnel. The courts of admiralty and chancery—both of England and of France—are in agreement: the tunnel cannot proceed without the rights to the Duchy of Aquatique."

"That so?" Dexter seemed distressingly uninterested in the fortunes of Lady Eleanor and her waterlogged dominion. "You know, I have some royal blood. A second cousin, thrice removed, Lord Timothy Dexter. I'm named for him."

"Indeed, sir? From which of England's shires?"

"Not England. Massachusetts. Newburyport, Massachusetts."

"I'd always been led to understand Americans shied from titles of nobility."

"Not this fellow. Had to give himself the title, but that was OK with him." Timothy Dexter's eyebrows echoed his amusement. "Being his namesake, I tried it on myself. But the wife and girl wouldn't go along."

"He that hath wife and children hath given hostages to fortune, for they are impediments to great enterprises."

"That's the real Sunday-school truth, that is. You have a nice way of putting things, Archie."

"Thank you, sir. Or, if I may take the liberty, *Your Lordship*."

"Yes, you may. Say, where does one get a drink on this tugboat?"

"The smoking saloon is, I believe, one deck above, and to the sternward."

"I think I'll venture forth. Tell my secretary... what the hell's the boy's name?"

"Tomasz, Your Lordship. Tomasz Szczęsny."

"Well, tell Tommy to bring me that letter there."

"Very good, Your Lordship."

There was an awkward moment while Archie attempted to remain in the cabin after the exit of his employer, but Lord Dexter's look of suspicion spooked the ersatz valet and future Viscount of Abernethy and he went off to his own cabin under the other's watchful eye.

There he found Tomasz petting his little moustache while he checked his work—only seven errors, and none of them he thought critical.

"His lordship wants you to bring that to him in the smoking saloon," Archie informed him.

"His lordship? *He's* a lord?"

"Not a real one. Thinks he inherited the title from

some ancestor more nutty than he is. He's made me a viscount. The Viscount of Abernethy."

"Should I call you both 'Your Lordship'?"

"Him only in private, me only after we reach New York."

Tomasz nodded as he left, but it was mere bravado. Things were not becoming clearer.

Once he was alone, Archie retrieved the sewing kit which also held his lock picks. He then spent a frustrating hour dodging stewards and battling a mounting anxiety as he endeavored to break into the cabin of Lord Dexter. Having failed, he returned to his own quarters and took out his flask, then drank to the eternal damnation of German craftsmanship.

And so, cherished reader, the principal players have been introduced. Our heroine, Mrs. Biddle (masquerading as Lady Eleanor Marsouin of Aquatique, but traveling as Elsbeth Duncan); her wayward attendant, Mélisande; the enigmatic Dowling, mastermind of the scheme; Tomasz, the dreamy Polish secretary; Lord Timothy Dexter, his eccentric American millionaire employer; and Archie Cobb, confederate of Dowling, valet to Lord Dexter, and only later assuming the title Viscount of Abernethy. Just six in all. Seven if we include baby Eugenia—though surely at this age more prop than player.

Rest assured, this will not be one of those excessively populated tales that so irritate the reader who strives to preserve his mind in its pristine state. There will be no long list of ancillary characters cluttering up the narrative. Police sergeants may dance about naked, and lavender-scented ladies pass all the salacious epistles they like. All will remain unnamed. Mere incidentals. On this, I give you my word.

3

With the aid of his flask, Archie Cobb regained his resolve. There could be no doubt, he reasoned, that Lord Timothy Dexter possessed an ample supply of reliable cash. Archie himself had taken the bank draft to the Lloyd line's ticket office and then been required to wait while inquiries were made at Lord Timothy's London bank—the cashiers of German steamship lines being as annoyingly painstaking as their locksmiths. With first-class cabins for both his lordship and his servants, not to mention the several dozen crates of newly acquired curios in the hold below, the total had come to nearly two hundred pounds sterling. No, there could be no doubt about it. Somehow—almost certainly by pure luck—Lord Dexter had come into the stuff.

It was now four o'clock and time for Archie to set the stage for the arrival of his compatriots. He went about the promenade deck listening for American accents, and when he found them, entered into friendly conversation. Sometimes he began by commenting on the weather, sometimes by offering a witty observation on the cramped accommodations. But he always ended by asking, sotto voce, if his listeners were aware that Lady Eleanor Marsouin would be boarding in Cherbourg.

"Of course, not under her real name," he confided. "Calling herself Elsbeth Duncan, pretending to be a Yank. I have that from the purser himself."

"What's this Lady Eleanor look like exactly?"

"Oh, you must have seen her photograph. Tall,

blonde. The real raspberry jam, she is. No mistaking *her*."

But Archie left off all mention of the Duchy of Aquatique. There was a limit, he suspected, to even an American tourist's gullibility.

At ten minutes to five, Mrs. Biddle and her party arrived at Cherbourg's Gare Maritime, the railroad depot which occupied a large pier projecting into the harbor. She placed what remained of the two hundred francs into an envelope and mailed it to the hostel in Étaples. Once she had brought Mélisande to New York, all her debts would be paid. But unless the scheme went off, she herself would arrive destitute.

As they neared the Lloyd line's tender—the small steamboat that would shuttle them to the *Kronprinz Wilhelm*—she gave Mélisande her instructions.

"A woman will approach me. It's her you must plant the watch on."

"*My* watch?"

"She means to take your place on the boat. Keep the watch, or come to New York. It's your choice."

Mélisande shrugged a reluctant assent. "What does she look like?"

"I don't know, but she will come towards me. Can you do this while carrying the baby?"

"*Mais oui*, she will make it easier."

"Once we separate here, stay as far from me as possible. Try not to even look in my direction. You board the boat first. The woman will be looking for me, but I won't board until I've drawn her off. You must plant the watch before she leaves the boat. Once she does, I will nod and your sergeant will arrest her. When we get out to the steamship, I will board first. A small, grey-haired man with a beard will be watching me. After he boards, you may. We'll meet in the cabin, that of Elsbeth Duncan. But I don't want anyone to realize we're together for as long as possible."

As she boarded the tender, Mélisande had an inspiration of her own. She began fussing over Eugenia in the obnoxious manner of a proud mother. As she expected, this drew the attention of the other passengers. All except one—a plump young woman whose eyes remained fixed on the gangplank. Mélisande began pacing, as if to pacify the child, then stumbled into the woman. Mrs. Biddle, who had only just started up the gangplank, looked back over her shoulder as if having forgotten to attend to something, then returned to the dock. The woman now bearing the watch of M. Bouc disembarked as if to follow her.

"Miss Duncan!" she called.

Mrs. Biddle stopped, turned toward her, then nodded. On cue, Eugenia's dancing partner emerged from the shadows and pulled the plump woman aside. Mrs. Biddle now boarded the tender and made her way to the bow. All in all, a perfectly timed bit of choreography.

Halfway to the roadstead and the rendezvous with the *Kronprinz Wilhelm*, the man calling himself Dowling sidled up beside her.

"That wasn't playing fair, my dear," he complained.

Mrs. Biddle said nothing, simply stared out to sea.

"Poor Céleste," he went on. "What was it you told the police?"

"I don't know what you're talking about. But if you're worried for your lady friend, take the tender back. I'm sure Cobb and I can get along."

"With no seed money? I think you flatter yourself,

my dear." It was meant as a slight, but he was the one left feeling the discomfort.

As the tender came alongside the steamship, dozens of heads leaned over the rails above, each hoping for a glimpse of the renowned Lady Eleanor. Then, when Mrs. Biddle graced them with a glance in their direction, Archie Cobb led her new converts in a rousing cheer. There was no mistaking true aristocratic blood.

Aware now that they were in the presence of a celebrity, the other passengers on the tender made way. According to the natural order, Lady Eleanor must be the first to board. Dowling, meanwhile, stood back and watched, hoping to ascertain who among the others was the maid of whom Mrs. Biddle had spoken.

The purser didn't recognize the name Elsbeth Duncan, nor had he heard the rumor she was really Lady Eleanor. But his refined sense of self-preservation told him this was a woman who would demand coddling, and no one could coddle like a purser of the Lloyd line. He personally saw her to her cabin.

Throughout dinner that evening, all eyes watched for the arrival of Lady Eleanor. But all eyes watched in vain. Mrs. Biddle and her party had their meal in their cabin, where they took turns enjoying their private bath. Later, the faux duchess gave her servant a detailed description of the scheme. Perhaps too detailed. Though by no means unintelligent, Mélisande's exposure to complex con games involving false imperial land grants and imaginary aristocrats had been limited. At the lecture's conclusion, she wasn't entirely sure whether her patron was pretending to be an American who happened to come into an underwater duchy, or a natatorial duchess emigrating to America. But it seemed a minor point and not worth suffering the inevitable sardonic remark by asking for clarification.

II

At midnight, with her daughter fed and Mélisande given explicit orders not to leave the cabin, Mrs. Biddle went off for a prearranged meeting. At 12:02, her contumacious retainer wrapped the infant in a blanket and carried her up to the boat deck, where they could both experience the open ocean for the first time.

They stood facing into a cool breeze—the girl laughing, the newborn, as usual, dumbstruck. A mere dozen feet away stood another passenger enjoying his first night on the open sea. Until their arrival, Tomasz had lost himself in the clear night sky, fashioning constellations of his own imagining. Now he turned his sights on Mélisande. Within minutes he constructed a rough outline of her life, and was filling in the blanks of what promised to be a three-volume Victorian novel when he was abruptly interrupted.

Mélisande had been swinging the baby about in a manner Tomasz thought cavalier for a mother and he was busily revising chapter seven to account for this odd behavior when the blanket loosened and Eugenia was launched into flight. Tomasz tossed aside his psychic pen and dove beneath the airborne child. Miraculously, he caught her just inches away from what looked like a lethal steel projection. Sadly, his own skull kept the appointment for her.

When he came to, Mélisande had his head in her lap and was stroking it tenderly. And the baby, which he still held to his chest, was staring up at him in a way that might have reminded those who knew him of Tomasz's own customary expression. He would have been content to remain locked in mutual wonderment with the child for as long as its mother stroked him, but a German officer coming upon the scene thought it too intimate for public display. He helped Tomasz up, and Mélisande took back her charge. When the officer had passed on, she thanked the child's savior for his timely assistance.

"Oh, I was pleased to help," he told her. "So thoughtful a baby."

"She thinks of only the one thing, her mama's milk."

Tomasz followed her look to where the baby was nestled and blushed.

"You're American, aren't you?" he asked, looking up.

"Yes, we come from... Pittsbourg." Thank goodness she'd paid attention when the Americans at Étaples spoke of home. "Pittsbourg, Philadelphia."

"Is Philadelphia a state?"

"Why not?"

"And your husband, he awaits you there?"

"No, he is dead. The Indians come and burn him up."

"How horrible."

"Yes, they are very mean, the Indians."

"So you travel to forget...." Tomasz was writing out loud.

"Forget what?"

"The cruel death of your baby's father...."

"Oh, yes. Very sad. But now we must go, or the witch will be angry."

"Witch?"

Mélisande gave him a kiss and vanished. Tomasz found a deck chair and sat down. He had a long night of revisions before him.

While her servant was giving the vacant Pole a lesson on American life, Mrs. Biddle conferred with Archie Cobb and the man currently calling himself Dowling in the latter's cabin.

"Why in heaven's name did you miss dinner?" Dowling asked sharply. "We need to work fast—we have just five days."

"I decided it was better to heighten anticipation. Dexter must come to me, after all."

"She's right," Cobb agreed. "Even he couldn't miss all the talk of Lady Eleanor."

"Can you describe him so I'll recognize him?" Mrs. Biddle asked.

"You won't have any trouble with that. Tall and thin as Banbury cheese, with snow-white hair down to his shoulders. Looks like your Uncle Sam—only, clean-shaven."

"Have you found out exactly how much he has?" Dowling asked him.

"No, won't let me near his things."

"I thought you were his valet?" Mrs. Biddle asked.

"So did I. Seems he mainly wants me to do some play acting when we get to New York, says he needs an English lord to impress his wife. And there's another bit of a complication. He had me hire him a secretary the day before we sailed."

"Damn! Why didn't you wire me?" Dowling demanded. "I could have called the whole thing off."

Archie chose not to admit that was precisely why he hadn't wired. What neither he nor Mrs. Biddle knew was that Dowling was bluffing. For his own reasons, he couldn't afford to call the scheme off.

"It's not as bad as it seems," Archie assured them.

"He left the hiring to me. His secretary is a Polish kid, as green as a leek. Knows nothing about money or business. And Dexter doesn't trust him either. Still, we might want to keep him occupied."

"I'll take care of that," Mrs. Biddle told them. They both looked at her as if awaiting elaboration. But she offered none. "So, how do we play it out?" she asked Dowling.

"Archie tells him about my role as buyer for the syndicate. We'll make sure Dexter sees me pestering you to sell, and sees some of the bundle I'm carrying. I'll get him in a card game and let him win some. Let him think I'm a dullard. In the meantime, you keep happening to bump into him. Then you confide in him."

"And the endgame?" she asked.

"An auction on the last night at sea. He and I bidding, and we make sure he can beat my last bid. So we must know exactly how much he has." He looked hard at Archie.

"Don't worry, I'll get in to see it one way or another."

"How much do you have?" Mrs. Biddle asked Dowling.

"After all the expenses, just over four thousand. During the auction, I'll agree that his man, Archie, hold the money. He can look through the bag, showing just enough to maintain the illusion. Dexter wins, you give him his deed, we make our split, and then go our separate ways. Agreed?"

Mrs. Biddle nodded, then left the cabin without another word. Dowling rose and poured out two large brandies.

"She's a hard one," Archie said. "And the way she talks to you? Can't seem to spare a kind word for her own father."

Good lord! Her own father? Well, treasured reader, no one is more surprised at this revelation than myself. But please understand, I am not the source of this chronicle, only its assembler. (A fuller explanation will be provided when time allows.) In order to preserve the story's freshness, I write as I glean. And it's only just now that I've gleaned this item of interest. In fairness, we all should have suspected they were family from the degree of loathing she's shown for him.

Mélisande returned to the cabin sometime after her mistress, and once Eugenia had been placed in her cradle, Mrs. Biddle slapped the defiant girl hard.

"*Never* take her from the cabin!"

"As you wish, madame. But why shouldn't little sister enjoy the air outside?"

Mrs. Biddle made as if to slap her again, but Mélisande stopped her, clasping her wrist in a surprisingly strong grip.

"Be careful, *madame*, or someday I will slap you back. And you will feel it for a very long time."

Mrs. Biddle knew she had gone too far in hitting the girl she still depended on. And the protest it had elicited reminded her of one she herself had made years ago in very similar circumstances. But there was no apologizing.

That night, Eugenia found herself unable to sleep and considered it a sound strategy to share the experience. At three o'clock, Mélisande put her finger on the problem. She went into the bath and opened each of the cocks just enough to provide a steady drip. Of course, this being a German ship, it was *a tropf... tropf... tropf...* that lulled Eugenia to sleep and not the *plic... plic... plic...* to which she'd grown accustomed during her stay in France. Thankfully, the young are free of linguistic prejudice.

III

The next morning after breakfast, Archie accompanied Lord Timothy Dexter to his cabin. Once again, he began straightening up. But whenever he neared the wardrobe, his lordship warned him off.

"Watch yourself, mister. Watch yourself."

Archie felt confident that he had at least ascertained where Dexter kept his loot. He now began setting up the next stage of the scheme.

"Wasn't Lady Eleanor looking radiant this morning, Your Lordship?"

"Radiant?"

"Aglow. Such a stunning woman. Yet one could see she was troubled. Something in her eye."

"Cinder?"

"Apprehension, I think, Your Lordship. She's being hounded by that syndicate we spoke of yesterday. Did you notice that man with the grey beard speaking with her?"

"Little fellow?"

"Yes, that's the one. He represents the syndicate planning to build the tunnel. He's made offers for her duchy, but she is clearly of a divided mind."

"Why's that? Why not take what she can get—can't be doing her any good at the bottom of the sea."

"True, sir. But perhaps the lady fears that the price offered is not commensurate with the deed's value to the syndicate—that this agent hopes to profit at her expense. One can't help but wonder if there isn't an opportunity here for a third party. Someone with both capital and a proper appreciation for the nuances of commercial dealings."

"You mean, get ahead of the syndicate's man and

buy the deed from her, then sell it to them at a nice profit?"

"That is precisely my meaning, Your Lordship. Such a person would profit both monetarily and spiritually, for he would ensure that Lady Eleanor received a fair price."

"Maybe so. Maybe so. But if it's too fair a price, there won't be any profit for the third party."

His employer's reply struck Archie as too ambivalent. Even his eyebrows seemed indifferent. No doubt another dose of Lady Eleanor's charm would bring them around. And all that was needed to administer it was to persuade Lord Dexter to go for a stroll on the promenade deck.

This was rather easily accomplished, as there are very few diversions on a steamship between breakfast and the noon hour, particularly for men of a speculative temperament. It is true that some small wagers are made at the morning meal. The New York newspaperman at table twelve felt certain enough that the next person entering the room would be a woman that he placed a silver dollar on the table at even odds. And the German salesman at table five offered seven to four that the odd-looking Englishman at table six would again lose his bridgework in his coffee. But it wasn't until afternoon that the gambling would get under way in earnest.

As Lord Dexter and his manservant rounded the bow of the promenade deck, they were stopped dead in their tracks—the way blocked by a buzzing hive of American tourists.

"Where bees are, there is honey," Archie offered.

"How's that?"

"I suspect if we make our way forward, we will come upon the object of adoration."

Archie pushed through the crowd with his curious employer following directly behind. It wasn't long before Lady Eleanor and Lord Dexter, both on the tall side, caught sight of one another. She offered him a tableau of besieged virtue peppered with forlorn hope, utilizing the pose she catalogued as Melancholia #9, which included a hand raised to the brow, palm outward. It had served her well in the past and it did so again. Lord Dexter was affected. His eyebrows arched upwards at the inside corners, forming a white chevron—the signal flag of a touched soul.

"Someone should extricate the poor woman from these buzzards," Archie suggested.

Lord Dexter, pushing past him, accepted the assignment.

His work completed, Archie made his way to the boat deck for some morning sun. When he emerged at the top of the stairs, he espied Dowling not far ahead. He was carrying a small brown leather bag, the sort doctors make use of. Archie felt compelled to follow. When Dowling entered the purser's office, he listened through an open porthole.

"I'd like to have this put in your vault," Dowling told the man at the counter.

"Very well, sir." The attendant took the bag and gave Dowling a chit in return. "You can retrieve it anytime between the hours of seven a.m. and eleven p.m."

Archie wandered off to the far side of the ship. Was it out of concern for *his* trustworthiness that Dowling felt it necessary to check his stash? Or that of his own daughter? It certainly couldn't have been the crew that worried the old man. Archie had never seen such a dutiful group in all his life. In fact, the assistant purser helping

Dowling was one of the most dutiful of all.

Mention was made earlier about the predilection for gambling on steamships. For those not interested in furthering their minds through reading, or buttressing their friendships through correspondence, there was little else to do. These sportsmen would bet on just about anything: cards, the weather, the ship's daily mileage, a human steeplechase, whether more people circle the promenade deck going clockwise or counter-clockwise, etc., etc. Needless to say, all this wagering opens up possibilities for men of flexible ethics. An adept can live high for a year on the take from one voyage. Such a man as the one currently calling himself Dowling.

It had been some years since he'd plied the steamship trade, and when he did, he had favored the British lines. But there had been one voyage to the Mediterranean via the Lloyd line when he was targeting an American banker traveling to Nice. It was a very lucrative voyage. Unfortunately, it was also the one on which this same assistant purser had initiated his career as a steward, third class.

Though confident in his memory, the assistant purser did not feel certain enough to risk confronting a passenger. To do so and be wrong would mean the end of his employment. But he would keep an eye on the little man.

By this time, the sun had risen just high enough to cast a revivifying ray upon the visage of the still-sleeping Tomasz. He woke groggily, and was giving his face a good rubdown when Archie came upon him.

"So this is where you spent the night."

"I came up for some air and must have fallen asleep. I suppose breakfast is over?"

"Yes, but why don't we see what passes for elevenses in the Vienna Café," Archie suggested. "This sea air certainly sharpens the appetite."

As the two entered the nearby café, Tomasz for the first time set eyes on Mrs. Biddle. She and Lord Dexter sat at a table, alone.

"Who's that with his lordship?" he asked.

"Lady Eleanor Marsouin, Duchess of Aquatique."

"She is very beautiful."

"Beauty may have fair leaves, but bitter fruit."

"Is she married?"

"No, but don't go setting your hopes on her, Tommy. She'd skin you alive."

Tomasz nodded absently.

4

The second afternoon at sea was spent variously as follows: Archie Cobb took a long nap in a deck chair, periodically disturbed by ball-playing children who used him as a target and thereby interrupted his dreams of tossing them to the sharks below; Lord Dexter joined a motley party at the stern-end of the promenade, where they ventured on the coloration of the next seagull to land on the afterdeck, the others apparently too inebriated to notice it was the same three birds coming and going; in the smoking saloon, the man currently calling himself Dowling labored to secure his claim on a rich vein of ill-guarded wealth he'd unearthed, using nothing save his bare hands and a cold deck; ever the playful soubrette, Mélisande distracted a member of the crew in the cabin she shared with the sleeping Eugenia and her absent mother; and while the duchess herself gave an audience near the shuffleboard court, a captivated Tomasz looked on, musing upon the flawless commingling of feminine form and pater-pleasing title.

When things broke up, Archie felt only partially rested, Tomasz's soul only partially sated, and the Duchess of Aquatique entirely exasperated. She had expected to resume her enthrallment of Timothy Dexter. Instead, a riveting matinee performance was wasted on a school of simpletons who ogled her dumbly like so many gaping fish.

The other half of our entourage fared better. Dowling's dexterity netted him eighty-seven dollars, while Lord Dexter's keenness at ornithological observation gained him three hundred and twelve, plus a gold watch that displayed the phases of the moon. And Mélisande's talents... well, discretion prevents me from revealing what transpired in cabin 176. Suffice it to say, she got exactly what it was she was after.

After dressing himself for dinner, Archie Cobb retrieved his employer's tailcoat from the laundry, where it had been thoroughly sponged. At the previous evening's meal, Lord Dexter had collected an arresting assortment of sauces and vintages. It was not at all unusual for his lordship's garb to serve as a sort of culinary blotting paper, providing a rough historical record of his last meal. In this case, reading from the bottom-most layer first, dinner began with something in a sauce Alexander accompanied by hock, followed by béchamel and champagne. Generous portions of both bordelaise and claret came next, then the whole was topped with chocolate and Madeira.

On entering Dexter's cabin, Archie found his lordship dancing on his bed. The attentive valet soon determined the cause of the upheaval: a gigantic insect. It skittered about the cabin, then stopped to hover just opposite Lord Dexter's face, inspecting him with huge insect eyes while its subject signaled his rejoinder via flexing eyebrows. Archie rolled up a magazine and began swinging.

"Stop, you fool!" Lord Dexter cried. "Can't you see that's a darning needle?"

"Darning needle, Your Lordship?"

Lord Dexter was referring to an insect of the suborder Anisoptera, more commonly known as the dragonfly. Archie's knowledge of entomology was, in the main, limited to the bedbugs, cockroaches, and houseflies of his native London. Though once, some twenty years before, he had been stung by a bee, or wasp, while visiting a cousin—his first and last excursion to the rural districts.

In due course, the insect made its own way out the open porthole, Lord Dexter peering after it.

"Am I to understand, Your Lordship, that these bugs hold some special place in your heart?"

"The first Timothy Dexter promised he'd come back as a darning needle."

"Ah, he was a theosophist, then?"

"How's that?"

"He believed in the mystical," Archie elaborated, while helping Lord Dexter into his tailcoat.

"I suppose you could say that. Had his own fortune-teller."

"Indeed?" Archie saw possibilities for the future. "He is wise that is ware."

"Where is he?"

"The other ware, Your Lordship, meaning vigilant."

"I see. Yes, I see," Lord Dexter fibbed.

Archie's thoughts now returned to the concerns of the present. He still needed to find Lord Dexter's stash. Once again, he tried to remain behind in the cabin on his employer's exit. And once again he was thwarted. More drastic steps would need to be taken after dinner.

Against his better judgment, Archie finished his entree quickly and skipped his dessert completely. He knew the result would be dyspepsia coupled with misery—for Archie truly relished his pudding. But he also knew this would be the ideal time to force his way into his employer's sanctum. He went to his own room, where he'd removed a steel brace from his cabin mate's bed. It was flat, with angled ends, and looked almost as if it had been intended to serve double duty as a jimmy. Archie pushed it up his sleeve, then crept toward his objective.

He had just positioned his makeshift crowbar for maximum effect when he heard something fall to the floor inside the cabin. He listened closely... silence... then someone moving about... then what sounded like the wardrobe being forced open.... Good God! Some freebooter was pirating the loot!

Instinctively, Archie banged on the cabin door with his jimmy. But not being a brave man, he returned his tool to his sleeve and ran off to summon a ship's officer. He found the assistant purser not far away looking already concerned.

"Come quick!" Archie shouted. "Burglary!"

When they reached the cabin, the door stood open. They entered cautiously—but too late. The culprit had fled.

"Is this your cabin?" the officer inquired.

"No, that of my employer, Lor... eh, Mr. Dexter."

"Can you say what might be missing?"

Archie looked about. "Some silver cuff links, I believe. And a ruby tie-pin."

"Wait here—I will go for the purser."

Once the officer had left, Archie went to the wardrobe and pulled open the door. At the bottom, beside an eclectic collection of footwear, was a small carpetbag. It had the simple sort of lock easily opened with the bit of wire men of Archie's persuasion always have about them. He reached in and pulled out a banknote. Examining the bag more closely, he found it reassuringly stuffed with others. He now estimated Lord Dexter's funds in excess of one hundred thousand dollars.

It was only a few minutes more before Lord Dexter

himself arrived, just long enough for Archie to have finished stuffing his socks with banknotes before quickly closing the bag.

"Caught!" his lordship shouted.

"Oh, no, sir. It was I who interrupted the thief."

Fortunately for Archie, the assistant purser arrived with his superior and verified his story. Lord Dexter made an inventory and noted that in addition to the silver cuff links and ruby tie-pin, a diamond bracelet of Parisian design and costing $5,000 had been taken. Had the others been looking his way, they would have seen the assistant purser swallow hard at this news—and then swallow hard again when the locksmith announced the door had been opened with a key.

It was Archie whom Lord Dexter had his eye on. He insisted his servant turn out his pockets and remove his jacket so the lining could be examined. It was then the makeshift jimmy fell to the floor.

"Came off the bed in my cabin," Archie explained. "I'd just gone off to tell the steward when I heard noises in here."

Lord Dexter said nothing, but his eyebrows spoke volumes.

II

The assistant purser accompanied Archie back to his cabin to look into the broken bunk. He was delightfully devoid of suspicion, offering to send round the ship's carpenter to make repairs. A few minutes later, a not-at-all-unsuspicious Lord Dexter arrived and insisted on searching the cabin. When he had gone, Archie sat down, wiped his brow, and pulled out the sheaf of banknotes that circled his left ankle. Seven one-hundred-dollar bills, and six more circled his right. The question now was, were they authentic? This was a matter outside Archie's expertise. Had they been British banknotes, he'd know just what to look for. But he seldom came across American greenbacks.

There were, however, two aspects of these greenbacks that concerned him. First, they weren't particularly green—in fact, not green at all, more of a pale apricot. And second, the ornate writing across the midsection read, "Confederate States of America." Though no student of political geography, this struck Archie as somehow anachronistic. He was beginning to comprehend the arithmetic that allowed Lord Dexter to turn a profit selling for three thousand dollars a steamboat for which he'd paid ten thousand.

Archie returned the notes to his stockings and took out his flask. He took a long draught and thought. Then he took a second, longer, draught and thought harder. What he needed was a plan. A plan that would allow him to maintain his cozy position with Lord Dexter, yet protect him from the vengeful Dowling. With the third draught, the solution seemed obvious: betray his confederates. But, and this was key, betray them without exposing himself. To do that, he would need a third party to act as his involuntary agent. Someone gullible enough to be easily manipulated, and yet someone Dowling would accept as a believable antagonist. Yes, of course. Tomasz. Tomasz must expose the plot. Then Dowling and his daughter would be content simply to avoid prosecution. They would be free to proceed to their next affair and Archie could go on to play the Viscount of Abernethy.

The great weakness in Dowling's scheme had always

been the ludicrous conceit on which it was based. If it was made clear that the duchy was purely imaginary, the plan would collapse. Tomasz must be made to discover—for himself—that Mrs. Biddle was a fraud.

While Archie went off looking for the vacant Pole, Lord Dexter entered the smoking saloon and began assessing which of the card games would prove the most profitable. He saw the little man he knew to represent the well-financed, tunnel-building syndicate sitting behind a tall mound of chips. The snow-white eyebrows danced a celebratory gigue.

Dowling rose and invited the simple-looking gentleman to join them. The others at the table readily acceded—millionaire eccentrics were always welcome, and Timothy Dexter was by now known to be both.

Over the next three hours, Dowling played the bumbler—making foolish bets, exposing his hands with transparent emotions, even misdealing. His intimidating mound of chips was reduced to a vulnerable ant hill. Meanwhile, Lord Dexter, in spite of his tell-tale eyebrows, seemed unstoppable.

But enough was enough. Dowling was determined, for a very sound reason, that the profits of the afternoon game not be sacrificed. He began playing in earnest. For the next half hour, he did himself well. But then, somewhere about the seventh whiskey and soda, Lord Dexter's eyebrows became cunning. They exhibited excitement at a pair of twos, and indifference at a flush. Instead of winning, Dowling was soon delving into the eighty-seven dollars he'd won in the afternoon session.

What made his lordship's eyebrows appear so cunning was that they had completely lost interest in the game. They had reached that state of inebriation where half-remembered anecdotes are exchanged to exaggerated amusement, and minor disputes quickly lead to harsh exchanges. It's oft said, an intoxicated eyebrow is an unpredictable eyebrow. And an unpredictable eyebrow is the poker player's friend.

As Dowling's stack shrank before him, behind his back Archie Cobb was endeavoring to betray him.

Archie found Tomasz observing the night sky from a deck chair and hailed him.

"Ah, there you are. I've been looking for you everywhere."

"Does his lordship need me?" Tomasz sat up and for the twenty-ninth time that day straightened his tie.

"If you mean, did he ask for you, no. But he needs you, my boy. He most assuredly needs you."

"What are you talking about?"

"I strongly suspect his lordship is being set up by a pair of confidence tricksters."

"Confidence tricksters?"

"Charlatans bent on relieving him of his money."

"Who?"

"For one, that phony duchess."

"Lady Eleanor? No, that I do not believe."

"I don't think there can be much doubt. You see, there is no Duchy of Aquatique."

"Who says there is no duchy?" Tomasz asked indignantly. "Since she is a duchess, there *must* be a duchy."

"Yes, but that's what I'm telling you. She is no duchess."

"Liar!" Tomasz rose and moved close to Archie. "And if you repeat that slander, I must insist we meet on the field of honor."

With that, Tomasz stomped off.

Archie sat down and wiped his brow. The foolish Slav had allowed his infatuation to cloud his thinking. And it seemed unlikely there was time enough to get the boy to see reason without provoking him to violence. Assuming he was capable of seeing reason at all.

By morning, the sea had turned rough and attendance at breakfast was sparse. Most of the passengers were staying as still as possible in their cabins. Hunger, and a bit of calm, brought many of them to the dining room for lunch. But then the weather worsened and back to their cabins they fled.

At three o'clock, Mélisande, who found the atmosphere of the cabin stifling when shared with her irritable mistress for any length of time, ventured to the reading room with the book that comprised her personal library, *The Girl Proposition*. Authored by a man named George Ade, and subtitled *A Bunch of He and She Fables*, it had been a parting gift from one of the American artists at Étaples. Study it well, he had told her, for Ade is to America what La Fontaine is to France. Mélisande had no idea what La Fontaine was to France, but she treasured the gift just the same.

She opened the book to the next lesson, or fable, which began: *Once there was a Social Fizzle named Homer Splivens. He was the dampest Fire-Cracker that ever tried to Pop.* Not only was Mélisande learning much about American rituals of courtship and marriage, she was also expanding her ready vocabulary.

III

While Mélisande read, Archie Cobb—who'd spent the morning and half the afternoon brooding over his dilemma—came to a decision. He would go to Dowling's daughter, bare his soul, and make a proposal.

Mrs. Biddle answered his knock by opening the door just wide enough to converse.

"It's rather important we have a little talk," he said.

She left him to wait in the passageway while she slid the cradle and the sleeping Eugenia into the bath. Only when she was satisfied that all trace of the child had been hidden did she allow Archie Cobb to enter. Her hard look did not make his task any easier.

"Might we sit down?" he asked.

"If you want." She cleared off two chairs.

"First, I'd like to ask about your relationship with your father."

"That's no concern of yours."

"No, certainly not. I only wish to know, are you acting for yourself, or for him?"

Mrs. Biddle made a little half-smile. "If you are asking, am I willing to sell out my father if it is to my advantage, the answer is a definite yes. You may rest assured, I can be every bit as venal as he is."

Though it was the answer he'd hoped for, Archie nevertheless felt chilled by the ease with which she gave it.

"Well, I suppose I need to begin by making a confession," he said nervously. "I've found Dexter's stash."

From his stocking, he drew one of the apricot-toned banknotes he'd taken from the carpetbag and handed it to Mrs. Biddle. Having seen from whence it came, she took it gingerly by a corner.

Her face hardened. Then, in a deliberate, ice-cold voice, she asked, "Are you telling me *this* is what he used to buy that steamship?"

"I fear so, yes." Archie was wondering if he hadn't made a mistake in thinking the daughter would be more sympathetic than her father. "My friend who sold it, Len Bailey, his eyesight isn't what it used to be. And besides, Len's always kept his mind on his business, never had much time for the politics of former colonies."

Much to Archie's relief, Mrs. Biddle laughed—a barely audible laugh, but a laugh nonetheless.

"This is priceless," she said. "I can't wait to see the old fool's face when he finds out."

"I was hoping we could see a way to avoid telling him, at least until we're off the boat."

"Yes, of course. But surely Dexter has *some* money with him. He wins every game he enters."

"He's got the goods, all right. I'm sure of that. But the old fox isn't easily snared. It might be easier to let him share it with us."

"How so? You aren't planning to remain his servant?"

"Serving him consists mostly of humoring him. He's not the sort who demands a lot of fussing. And there may be a position for you."

"What position?"

"He's the descendant of another Timothy Dexter. Lived in Massachusetts, sometime in the past."

"Of course, Lord Timothy Dexter."

"You've heard of him?"

"He was a celebrity around the turn of the last century. Wrote an absurd little book, *A Pickle for the Knowing Ones*. He spelled phonetically and made no use of punctuation at all. Until the second edition, when he added a page of marks at the end," Mrs. Biddle interrupted herself with another barely audible laugh, "then told the reader to salt and pepper them about as he wished."

"How quaint." Unlike Mélisande, Archie cared little for literature written in the American vernacular. "Well, our Dexter has likewise taken to calling himself Lord. Thinks his forebear visits him in the form of a giant insect. And yesterday he told me the first Lord Dexter had his own fortune-teller."

"Are you suggesting I offer him my services as soothsayer?"

"I was thinking of something more grand—say, court theosophist."

"I suppose that might be amusing. But I have my own plans."

"And landing without capital won't inconvenience you?"

"It would inconvenience me a great deal, were I to allow that situation to occur." Mrs. Biddle became thoughtful. "There is another source available, especially if you and I are pooling our efforts...."

"Your father's four thousand?"

"Why not? He'd do the same to either of us, wouldn't he?"

"Yes, I suppose he would," Archie agreed. "But I think he already suspects. Yesterday I saw him check a bag with the purser. Asked that it be put in the vault."

"That doesn't matter. All we need do is turn the auction around. Make sure *he* wins instead of Dexter. I take his four thousand, split it with you, and off we go."

"You don't think your old papa will sit still for that, do you? He must have iron nails who scratches a bear."

"We'll need to find some way to keep him in check. But we can work out the details later. For now, we should just make as if all is going according to plan. Tell him you've seen the money. How much was it?"

"Of this? A hundred thousand, at least," Archie told her. "I must say, I feel a great sense of relief from our talk."

Mrs. Biddle was about to respond when she was summoned to the bath by her daughter.

The secret revealed, she returned with the child in her arms.

"Not a word about her to anyone, particularly *him*. Understood?" Mrs. Biddle demanded.

"Yes, if that's how you want it. Well, good-bye, and good luck to us both."

Archie was not a sentimentalist, but there was something disheartening about a daughter wanting to hide her baby from its grandfather. Though in this case, perhaps, the caution was not unwarranted.

That evening, Mrs. Biddle set Mélisande onto the task of distracting Tomasz—a not too difficult undertaking given his disposition and the girl's complementary talents. She described the vacant Pole and Mélisande assured her she knew the young man—but wisely made no mention of their encounter on the boat deck two nights before.

"A very innocent boy," she said. "He reminds me of the virgin priest I won."

"What virgin priest did you win?" Mrs. Biddle asked.

"The only virgin priest we ever met. We, the girls of my town, drew lots for him. I won, so that night..."

"You tell such tales."

"It is no tale, madame. I don't see what's so strange about it—the priests drew lots for the girls when they came of age."

Mrs. Biddle shook her head, trying to hide a smile.

"Where is it that you met all these lecherous priests, Thélème?"

"No, in Arras. I don't know why you should not believe it," Mélisande went on. "When I told Jimmy Egan, he told me in Chicago the priests draw lots for the boys—only, they don't wait."

5

Throughout the voyage, Mrs. Biddle and her hand-maiden alternated attending meals in the dining room. When one dined publicly, the other ate in the cabin. In this way the baby was never left alone.

The third morning at sea, Mélisande went off to breakfast bearing a note for Tomasz. She passed it to a waiter and requested it be delivered anonymously. The smitten Pole wasted no time in opening the envelope that bore the scent he recognized as that of the Duchess of Aquatique.

M. Szczęsny,

I hope you will forgive my presumption in contact-ing you in this way. However, I feel I am at risk, and find myself without friends. There is one aboard who wishes me harm. For safety's sake, I dare not write more, but perhaps you could visit me in my cabin at ten o'clock this morning.

Yours, in desperation,
Lady Eleanor

Tomasz felt he had a very good idea as to the identi-ty of the Cretan bull to whom Lady Eleanor alluded. The man sitting just beside him, Archie Cobb. Though it was only half past eight, and his meal barely begun, Tomasz left the room lest his emotions get the best of him. This was not the time to strike, but to prepare for the trial ahead. And for Tomasz, preparing for any sort of trial involved a lengthy mulling of probabilities. So he went now to the boat deck and mulled.

At nine o'clock, Mélisande returned from breakfast and Mrs. Biddle went off to a prearranged meeting in Dowling's cabin. She found him already in conference with Cobb.

"Archie's confirmed that Dexter has at least a hundred thousand in cash," the man currently calling himself Dowling told her.

"And it's certain none are queer?" Mrs. Biddle asked.

Archie felt sure she was merely deflecting Dowling's suspicions with a display of her customary skepticism, but he would have preferred that it not come accompanied by her customary piercing stare.

"Yes, yes, of course," he stammered. "Absolutely."

"I saw a good deal of it last night at the card table," Dowling said. "It was real enough. How far have you gotten with him?"

"Only just started," Mrs. Biddle replied. "I've told him you've offered me ten thousand, but that I think it's worth more."

"Keep at him. Tell him I've raised the offer to twenty."

"Where's he now?" she asked Archie.

"In his cabin. Having the lock changed, for the third time."

"Lock changed? Does he suspect you?" Dowling asked.

"He suspects everyone, the wily old coot. But Thursday evening he was burglarized."

Archie hadn't intended to reveal this news, but having mentioned the repeated changing of the lock, an explanation was required.

"And the money not taken?" Mrs. Biddle asked incredulously, thereby causing Archie to wish anew that her thespian ambitions were more modest.

"I interrupted the thief. He only had time to take some jewelry."

"Who was it?" Dowling asked.

"Got away while I was fetching an officer."

"You're sure this burglar hadn't time to see the money?" Mrs. Biddle asked.

"Yes, the bag was locked. I had to pick it open," Archie explained.

"Go now and keep Dexter in the cabin," she told him. "It will be much easier if I can corner him there."

When Archie had gone, and his daughter had risen to do likewise, Dowling stopped her.

"I've determined who your maid is."

"That couldn't have been much of a challenge given that we share a cabin."

"Better keep an eye on that girl," he said.

"Are you attempting to menace me, old man?"

"Only some friendly advice. I saw her flirting with an officer the other afternoon. A girl like that can be trouble."

His last sentence was delivered to the closing door.

Back in her own cabin, Mrs. Biddle instructed Mélisande to keep the appointment with the Polish secretary and see that he remained until at least eleven, but not past noon.

Archie, meanwhile, had found Lord Dexter in his cabin speaking with the assistant purser, while supervising the replacement of the lock.

"It's that man Dowling, sir," the officer said. "I've noticed you have been gambling with him. I feel I've seen him before. Under a different name, and under circumstances that do him no credit."

"You think it was him that broke in?" his lordship asked.

"No, I fear... ah, no, that is not likely. But I do think he is the same card sharp who made off with a large sum of money belonging to another American on a voyage some years back. It may be I am wrong, but I thought it my duty to caution you."

To the bewilderment of the assistant purser, Lord Dexter smiled, while above, his eyebrows performed a lively courante. The officer made a short bow and exited with the locksmith.

Archie tried to repair the damage.

"Doesn't it seem rather improbable, Your Lordship, that the same man who plies steamships as a card sharp would be hired by a syndicate of moneyed Londoners for so delicate a task?"

"You're asking me if a gang of swindlers would hire a smooth-talking charlatan to bamboozle a lady out of her property? Think about it, man. Think about it."

His valet was relieved by Lord Dexter's interpretation and was about to voice approval when interrupted by a knock. He opened the door to Mrs. Biddle, announced Lady Eleanor, then discreetly left the cabin.

Interestingly, our heroine herself had not yet determined which part she would be playing. What she did know was that she could not get Dexter to the auction by executing the original scenario. For if she *did* manage to gain his sympathy, he would hardly be likely to do something so unsympathetic as offer bogus money for her deed.

She had devised two alternative strategies. Both

would require the collaboration of the fickle Lord Dexter. And both would end with the impoverishment of Dowling—an outcome she'd only first considered the day before, but one which had grown so far in her affection it had become a prerequisite.

The first strategy was to reveal the scheme in its entirety—including her own part in it—and then suggest she and Dexter collude to defraud Dowling. This plan held one minor inconvenience and one major risk. The minor inconvenience was that it would mean betraying the betrayal she had arranged with Cobb the previous afternoon. The major risk was that Dexter might prefer to expose them all rather than take a chance at what was likely to him a trifling sum.

The second strategy was to persuade Dexter to help the destitute duchess get the better of the unscrupulous syndicate and its deceitful representative. This plan would take advantage of the groundwork already laid, but it entailed one minor inconvenience and one major leap of faith. The minor inconvenience was that it would mean *not* betraying the betrayal she had arranged with Cobb the previous afternoon—since his abetment would be essential—and therefore having to share the profits with him. The major leap of faith was the same one on which the original scheme depended: that Dexter accept the faux duchy as genuine.

To decide between the two strategies, Mrs. Biddle had settled on a simple test of his lordship's credulity. She would show him her deed.

"Forgive me for intruding. But I find myself in need of someone I can trust."

"Well, don't look for him on this boat. A damnable den of thieves."

"Have you been robbed of some valuable?"

"A bracelet I bought for my daughter. A five-thousand-dollar Par-ee-shen bracelet. And a ruby tie-pin the girl gave me as a present. And a pair of cuff links, dills."

"Dills?"

"Had pickles carved on them."

"Ah. How horribly exasperating for you," Mrs. Biddle commiserated. "Perhaps I shouldn't be bothering you about my dilemma."

"Hell, girl, my whole life is one long chain of exasperations. Nothing new about that. You go ahead and sit down and empty your soul." Lord Dexter removed a stack of papers from a chair, but himself remained standing.

"That man I've told you about, Dowling, he now tells me he will give me twenty thousand dollars."

"Doubled it that quick? Then you ought to ask for fifty," he told her.

"I could so use the money. But I can't bear to part with this, my family's legacy." She reached in her bag and brought out the antiqued deed to the Duchy of Aquatique, then handed it to Lord Dexter. If he laughed out loud, she would as well—then execute strategy number one by telling him all about the scheme.

His lordship did not laugh, but held the document tentatively, gazing upon it as he would a sacred text. He knew not a word of Latin, and the name Charlemagne brought no light of recognition. But he found the crisp, yellowed parchment and red-wax seal not just credible, but convincing. And when he sighted the geographically distorted map on the reverse, his snow-white eyebrows shot northward. Strategy number two it would be.

"I feel certain this man Dowling and the syndicate

mean to take advantage of my situation," she confided. "I only wish there were a way to... I believe the expression is 'to turn the tables.'"

"Swindle the swindlers?" his lordship asked, the eyebrows temporarily inscrutable.

"I hope you won't find it presumptuous of me to suppose you might approve of such a course. It's only... I've heard a rumor, and coupled with your mention of the cuff links—dills, of course... might you be a descendant of *Lord* Timothy Dexter?"

"His namesake, even. You heard of him, have you?"

"Oh, yes, of course. The Pantagruel of the Merrimack. You may count me among those who regard his *Pickle* the American answer to *Tristram Shandy*."

"Quite so, quite so." His lordship couldn't recall the question this Tristram fellow had posed, but he preferred not to reveal his ignorance before a Knowing One. "He cut that Shandy down to size. Yes, ma'am."

"What's more, he was a man of commercial genius, and one who never hesitated to engage the hypocrites."

"Fought the hypocrites his whole life," his descendant agreed. "Not to mention the damnable bloodsuckers."

"Indeed. That's why I thought you might be receptive to helping me get the better of these... bloodsuckers."

Lord Dexter emitted a raspy cackle, while his eyebrows, having shed their apparent apathy, provided a visual accompaniment of wave-like oscillations.

Assuming this to be an answer in the affirmative, Mrs. Biddle continued. "I wonder... Forgive me if this suggestion seems a foolish one, but I wonder if it wouldn't help things along if I were to tell Dowling *you* had offered me fifty thousand dollars for the deed?"

"Bid him up?"

"Yes, but in the end, through some sort of sleight of hand, I manage to take his money, yet keep my legacy." The lady now stopped to fan herself. "I wonder if we could continue our discussion on the promenade? It's rather airless in here."

Mrs. Biddle knew it was Dowling's habit to go for a morning walk, and it was important that he remain convinced that things were proceeding as planned. When they reached the open deck and she espied him some way off, she brought him to Lord Dexter's attention.

"Do you think we could give him a little performance? Let him hear you offer me fifty thousand dollars?"

His lordship embraced the suggestion, and then delivered a quite respectable, if somewhat overly theatrical, performance. Histrionic eyebrows are an actor's friends— but not when they step on his lines.

II

While her patroness was working her charms on Lord Dexter, Mélisande was attempting the same with Tomasz. He had arrived anticipating a private encounter with Lady Eleanor and was visibly disappointed to find instead the baby-tossing American widow he'd met that first night on the boat deck.

"Excuse me, please. I must have the wrong cabin."

"No, no." Mélisande pulled him toward her and closed the door. Then, by pressing her body against his, she herded him further into the room. Each time she sallied, he retreated. But given the confines of a steamship cabin, it took only half a dozen sallies to have him pinned beneath her on the bed.

She had met resistance before, but strength of character has little chance against animalistic urgings when a shapely young girl has one pressed beneath her and is tickling one's ear with her very capable tongue. When Tomasz broke out in a sweat, she took it as encouraging. When his face turned a purplish-red, she read it as an extreme form of passion. But when he began foaming at the mouth and moaning in a decidedly unromantic way, she recognized it as a seizure.

She fetched a glass of water and began sprinkling his face. Soon he recovered enough to stumble to the safety of a chair, and not long after, the hyperventilating abated. But each time she came within a foot of him, the moaning began anew.

"Are you sick?" she asked.

"No, I don't think so. But please, I am a *gentleman*."

Mélisande had no idea what bearing that had on the matter but was loath to show her ignorance. "Ohhh. I did not know."

"I came at the request of Lady Eleanor." He took out the note she'd sent him and handed it to Mélisande.

"Yes, yes. I know. But she asked me to see you. She is very busy."

"Are you her friend?"

Mélisande emitted a noise signaling her ambivalence. "We travel together. She's American also."

"I thought the duchy was in France?"

"Yes, but she lives in America. Her grand-papa dies, she gets her duchy."

"What about her father?"

"Dead."

"Indians?"

"Ummm, no. He shoot his self."

"Suicide? Why?"

"Because mother, she sleeps with grand-papa." Mélisande had a knack for creating biographies.

"Poor Lady Eleanor," Tomasz said, shaking his head. "Do you know who it is who threatens her?"

"Threatens her? No. Do you like her?"

"Oh, yes. Very much. She is the most beautiful-looking woman I've ever met."

"Yes," Mélisande agreed reluctantly. "But if you *only* look."

Tomasz hadn't heard her addendum. "Do you think she feels the same about me? I mean, that she likes me?"

"Oh, sure. Didn't she send you a note?"

"I'd like to send her one. Telling her how much I care for her."

"Why not?"

"Would you help me to write it?"

"Sure, OK. I am very good making love letters." She cleared a space on the small table, then set out pen, ink, and paper. "I will tell you what to write."

Tomasz had hoped to use the specimen the German lady who smelled of lavender had handed him as a template. But when he translated the first paragraph for her, Mélisande dismissed it, holding her nose while making a sound of extreme distaste.

"No, no. We do much better. Now, the object," she explained, "is to nail the girl without giving her a chance to become acquainted or investigate." This advice was taken directly from *The Girl Proposition*. She had known that someday Mr. Ade's treatise on American romance would prove useful, but never expected it to be so soon. Luckily, she had circled the choicest bits so they'd be easy to find. Now all that was needed was to string them together. "This is what you will write: *Dear Peacherette with the Kentucky Shape*...."

Here Tomasz stopped her to ask for clarification. She showed him the circled text and then they continued—she providing the vocabulary, and he adjusting the grammar—until finally arriving at this:

My Dearest Peacherette, You of the Kentucky Shape,

From the moment you crossed my pathway, I was stung in eight different places. You make Cleopatra look like Martha the sewing girl, and Venus arising from the sea, only squizzly old soap. You have a pair of incandescent headlights, a complexion like the sunset blush on a snowbank, and enough hair above for two girls your size.

Dare I crave a word from those rosebud lips, and hope for a melting glance from those starlit lamps? I would very much like to execute a clutch swing into the slow and dreamy.

The chickadees who chew gum on the trolley, and the mopey ones who wear wrappers and eat pickles, and the spindly ones in rainy day skirts, they are purty fair. But you make them look like the odds and ends of a rummage sale, in your exceptionally Gibson shirtwaist. I reach out my hot tentacles, O queen of the human race.

The love microbe is all through my system. The fires of passion have got beyond control and it is time to call out the whole department. I want you so hard I look in the porthole of your boodwar at night and gnaw the palings of the front fence. It is the essence of googoo, double strength.

Your omnibus of love...

They read it aloud to each other several times and while Mélisande insisted it was the real Latin Quarter article, Tomasz felt sure it wanted for something—the something that the lover of the lavender-scented German lady had expressed so well in his very stimulating penultimate paragraph. Too embarrassed to attempt a translation himself, he showed Mélisande the German original. When it became clear its meaning was lost on her, he tried to convey it via complex metaphor—the word "vessel" taking the place of the principal referent. What resulted, after much confused input by his coauthor, was an ode to glassware. Tomasz added it as a postscript.

"You will give this to your friend, the duchess?"

"Oh, sure. I will give it to her."

"And tell her, I am always at her service. And that I love..."

"Yes, yes." Mélisande was beginning to find his misdirected devotion vexing. It was now past the hour of noon, so she hurried him on his way.

Later that afternoon, while catching some sun on the boat deck, Mrs. Biddle encountered an anxious Dowling.

"Enter into a conversation with me," he whispered.

"Why? What's going on?"

"There's an assistant purser who's been watching me. Thrown me off my game—I had to leave the table."

"I don't see why I should assist you in fleecing your fellow passengers at the card table."

"Don't you? Well, if you want this scheme to come off..." He left his sentence unfinished, then changed the topic. "I heard Dexter offering you fifty thousand. I think it's time now to arrange the auction. I'll confront him and suggest it."

"No, it will be better if I tell him you proposed it. He needs to be handled very carefully."

An officer passed and eyed them, not at all subtly. Mrs. Biddle noticed Dowling tense.

"So that's your assistant purser? How did he know what you were up to?"

"No idea. The fools at the table seem clueless. Well, I had better get back to it."

Mrs. Biddle was now left to her thoughts, and her first thought was not a pleasant one. It dated back to Dowling's suggestion a few moments earlier that the success of the scheme somehow depended on his success at the card table. She could think of only one explanation: he did not have the four thousand dollars he had claimed or anything like that. And so, her reasoning continued, his checking of the bag wasn't to keep his bankroll safe from the others, but to keep them from learning he had no bankroll. In all likelihood, the old buzzard knew Cobb was observing him when he sent it to the vault. Now he was frantically trying to raise the seed money. The money she had set her sights on. Once again, she would need to revise her strategy.

I am sure, precious reader, that you will not be surprised to learn that Mrs. Biddle has deduced correctly. She is, after all, herself a virtuosa of deceit. And I hope you will find it in your heart to forgive me for having neglected to mention an episode that transpired three days earlier which sheds some light on the situation. It's just that it's been such a chore trying to keep it all straight. You honestly wouldn't believe what I have to contend with. But this is hardly the place to voice complaints.

It all began prior to Dowling and his lady friend, Céleste, leaving the Hôtel de l'Aigle. Céleste had never thought much of Dowling's scheme, or, indeed, of Dowling himself. But she did think a great deal of his four thousand dollars. While Dowling was meeting with Mrs. Biddle in the hotel's lobby, she was upstairs in room 517 replacing his four thousand dollars with cut-up strips of newspaper. Her plan was to board the tender with him, then exit at the last possible moment. When she had disembarked after approaching "Miss Duncan," it was her intention to keep on walking, into the Gare Maritime and onto the 5:23 express to Paris.

Because Dowling understood that Mrs. Biddle had engineered Céleste's arrest, he didn't realize that his money had been stolen until he opened his bag the next morning. And by then, they were well out to sea.

My, my, what a tangled web of intrigues....

6

It was late on a grey, but calm, Sunday morning and Archie Cobb's thoughts had fixated on the Vienna Café's pastry cart. He'd just made his way through a small knot of Calvinists indulging in a service *en plein air*, which at that moment meant fog and drizzle, when he saw a man leaving the purser's office with a small brown leather bag. A bag seemingly identical to that recently checked in by his confederate Dowling.

This one belonged to the lavender-scented German lady. She used it as a travel case for the exquisite collection of jewelry her once-devoted husband had lavished on her—the very man who had just retrieved it from the purser's vault. I say "once-devoted" because more recently suspicion had taken the place of devotion. He suspected his wife was having an affair with an artist of her acquaintance, and he further suspected written evidence of the affair had been hidden amongst her jewelry. He was correct on both counts, as he would have soon learned had he not been startled into dropping the bag by the first blast of the fog-horn.

He turned to retrieve it, but just as he did his wife called to him. She was herself suspicious and had followed him up to the boat deck, though not in time to see that he had already taken possession of the bag.

"What are you doing up here in the rain, my dear?" she asked.

"Just getting some air—feels quite refreshing, don't you think?"

"But you'll catch your death of a cold. Come back down, please. I'm so lonely by myself." She took his arm and gave him a look he'd not once resisted in seven years of marriage.

"You go, dearest, and I'll be down in a little while. Just a few minutes more."

"Then I'll stay with you...."

They had reached a stalemate. He was afraid to reveal that he suspected his fetching little wife until he was sure his suspicions were warranted, and so dared not retrieve the bag a few feet behind him. She was afraid to leave lest he reclaim the bag she thought still in the purser's vault, and her mad but doubtless transitory affair be exposed.

Archie, however, was under no such inhibitions. The fog had thickened and he crept silently toward his prey. When the horn next blew and the lavender-scented lady jumped into the arms of her husband, Archie seized both moment and bag. In a quick succession of cat-like bounds, he crossed to the far side of the boat and made his way down to the upper cabin deck.

There he came upon Mrs. Biddle just returning to her compartment. She looked down at the brown leather bag.

"Dowling's?" she asked softly.

"No, but just like it." Archie looked back over his shoulder. "Perhaps we can discuss it inside?"

She led him in and closed the door. Seeing Eugenia fast asleep in her cradle, she looked in the bath and found Mélisande immersed in the tub. They exchanged a brief word, then she closed that door and turned to Archie with a finger over her lips.

"I saw a fellow drop it up on the boat deck," he whispered. "I thought it might come in handy."

"You think the old man would fall for a switch?" she asked.

"If it's done with the proper finesse. And he has no reason to suspect it. Suppose while I have both his and Dexter's bags, I do the switch. We let Dexter win the auction, and your father leaves the room with this, thinking all's gone as planned."

"But how much time does that gain us?"

"Not much, perhaps. But if we just declare Dowling the winner, and you take his bag, well, in the heat of the moment..."

"You don't think he'd come armed?" she asked.

"It would be uncharacteristically crass, but your father's talents aren't what they were. And when men find themselves in that situation, they often resort to expediencies. Fear the worst, I say, the best will save itself."

"I suppose you're right," she agreed. "What's in the bag?"

"I haven't had time to look."

Archie set it on the floor and removed an oblong jewelry box which he placed on the table. Mrs. Biddle raised the lid, then fondled a string of perfectly matched pearls. She replaced these, then opened each of three drawers. The first held several rings and bracelets of various stones and settings, and nothing that wasn't of value; the second, a Henri Vever filigree brooch and three finely crafted pendants, at least one a Falize; and the final drawer, a dozen pairs of earrings, carefully selected to complement the rest.

"Any of it real?" Archie asked.

"If I say no, you'll only assume I'm lying."

"Well, perhaps we can split them, along with the four thousand?"

"Yes, perhaps. In the meantime, it might be best if they remain with me."

Archie wasn't sure that would be for the best. But as he preferred not to be seen carrying the bag he'd so recently purloined, and knew there was no telling when his distrustful employer might again search his cabin, he acquiesced.

"There's something else," she said. "And it concerns the old man's four thousand. I can't be sure, but I believe he may have been boasting."

"What do you mean?"

"Just something he said. He implied he needed to win at the table for the scheme to go off."

"But then why check the bag?" Archie asked. Then it dawned on him. "Oh, I see. To keep us from finding out he was broke.... Well, at least I still have my position with Dexter. He that serves, is preserved."

"Let's not give up on Dowling yet. He may still be capable of raising a good sum if he has the proper set-up. As I recall, you used to be quite an admirable steerer."

"Fatten him for slaughter? Yes, all right. I'll see what I can do. There certainly is no shortage of rich fools on the boat. And perhaps you can keep Dexter entertained—he's been winning something fierce. The man's luck only seems to run one way."

"All right," she agreed. "I'll take care of his lordship."

II

Once Archie had gone, Mrs. Biddle lifted the jewel box to return it to the bag and discovered a letter nestled in the hollowed bottom. She'd only just removed it when she heard the bathtub draining. Quickly, she put it with the box in the brown leather bag, and then placed that in the one piece of luggage Mélisande had been ordered to keep out of. This was normally kept locked, but Mrs. Biddle had made sure her light-fingered retainer had had one opportunity to search it and so convince herself it contained nothing of value.

The baby stirred and her mother picked her up and brought her to the bed. While Eugenia dined, her provisioner noticed her diaper had been fastened with a tie-pin. A ruby tie-pin. As the meal was concluding, Mélisande entered the room buffing herself with a towel.

"Where's the bracelet?" her mistress demanded.

"What bracelet, madame?"

Mrs. Biddle placed her now-sleeping child in the cradle and removed the tie-pin. She held it up to her recalcitrant servant's face. "The one you found in the same cabin as this."

"I don't remember any bracelet."

"You little fool, you've put everything at risk. I may have no choice now but to turn you over to them."

Mélisande made her usual show of nonchalance, but she sensed that this was something more than mere threat. She sauntered playfully over to the crib. With one hand she lifted the baby to her mouth and kissed her, while the other hand retrieved a diamond bracelet buried in the linen below.

"It was a gift, for little sister."

"How'd you get a key?"

"Oh, that was very easy. My friend, Oskar. He gave it to me."

"Your friend, Oskar?"

"*Mais oui*, he is an officer."

Mélisande was still dressing when Mrs. Biddle answered a knock at the door. It was the assistant purser.

"Might I have a word, madame?"

Mélisande, still no further dressed than her undergarments, rushed forward and embraced him. "Oskar! *Mon chéri!*"

The reddened assistant purser untangled himself, then closed the door. Once again he addressed Mrs. Biddle. "I believe, madame, that on a previous visit, I lost a key in your cabin."

"Did you indeed? Might I ask the nature of that visit?"

"The young lady... she requested that I help her...."

"Never mind what she told you. And I won't ask what went on. You may have your key." Mrs. Biddle turned to Mélisande. "Give it to him."

The girl shrugged, then pulled the key from a shoe beneath her bed and handed it to a grateful Oskar. He thanked them and made to leave, but Mrs. Biddle stopped him.

"I suppose you know what use she made of it?"

Oskar had been trying very hard *not* to know what use she made of it. But the recent series of jewel thefts kept intruding on his delusion.

"I understand Mr. Dexter lost a very valuable bracelet," Mrs. Biddle went on.

"Ja, yes, that is true. Did you... That is, do you know..."

"How would you like to capture the thief?"

Oskar looked at Mélisande, and she in turn looked at her mistress.

"Forget the girl. She knows nothing. But if you cooperate, before we dock in New York, you will have the thief and the jewelry—including some that has yet to be reported missing."

"Has yet to be reported missing?"

"Yes, but it's safe. Simply do as you are told and you'll appear the hero, rather than the accomplice."

"What do I need to do, madame?"

"For now, the man Dowling, leave him alone."

"Very well, madame. And when will you give me the jewelry?"

"I will not give it to you. You will discover it on the thief. Tomorrow night. You'll receive fuller instructions later. Now you may go."

Oskar made a slight bow and exited.

Mrs. Biddle turned to her servant. "You've been lucky this time, but don't count on that luck holding. I've no experience of the French jails, but I can assure you, you would not find your stay in a New York jail pleasant. The very things that enable you to appear so clever on the outside will mark you as prey on the inside. You need to learn your limits. Now I must go."

This time Mélisande held her tongue and accepted the admonishment with a sheepish grin. Mrs. Biddle left the girl wondering how she could both despise and admire her mistress in equal measure. Though often she felt like strangling her in her sleep, she was, nonetheless, thankful to be apprenticed to so cunning a master.

She was also thankful that no mention had been made of the cloisonné brooch she'd taken from cabin number 12, or the gold earrings, each with a teardrop pearl and a tiny green stone, contributed by the resident of cabin 121. And no doubt the woman in 153 was thankful that the thief who rifled her cabin didn't favor the heavily jeweled rings she herself did.

But at that moment, it was Tomasz who was most thankful. He'd just spent the better part of an hour taking down one of Lord Dexter's incomprehensible letters. This one apparently asking a tailor in New York to prepare an admiral's uniform of unique specifications. Now, at last making his exit, Tomasz turned to find his adored duchess in the passageway.

"Lady Eleanor! I answered your plea for help, but..."

"Yes, I am sorry I missed your call." The earnest secretary would need a new distraction. And why not kill two birds with one stone? "Are you still willing to help?"

"Oh, yes, of course, my lady. Anything."

Mrs. Biddle drew him into a side corridor and whispered, "There is an officer of the ship, the assistant purser. He is an impostor. In truth, he is none other than the infamous Oskar, an anarchist, and assassin, hired by my enemies."

"They mean to do you harm?"

Consummate actress though she was, Mrs. Biddle had difficulty masking her tone of contempt. "One generally doesn't hire an assassin to spread good cheer."

"Do not fear, Lady Eleanor. I, Tomasz Szczęsny, will confront this Oskar."

"No, that would be precipitous. For now, just watch him. Don't let him out of your sight."

"Very good, madame." Tomasz bowed and began to leave, but then turned back. "Did you receive my letter?"

"Letter? No, what was it about?"

"I, er... perhaps you could ask your traveling companion? I left it with her."

Tomasz rushed off. The thought of recounting the letter directly to the object of his adoration—particularly the postscript—unnerved him.

III

Mrs. Biddle gave Lord Dexter's door a knock and was given the habitual permission to come forth. She did so.

"I'm happy to report that Dowling has taken the bait. I told him of your offer—which he had, of course, overheard—and he suggested an auction. The deed will be sold to the highest bidder."

"Auction?" Lord Dexter made no effort to hide his dislike for the word. He preferred to buy what others disdained, and then find ways to profit from their sale. Things such as steamships mired in the Thames, or the banknotes of a lost cause.

"You need have no anxiety," Mrs. Biddle went on. "Your money will never be at risk. I will tell Dowling that you have agreed, provided your valet acts as auctioneer. Both sides will put up money, but only some small portion need be visible. We will make sure you win the auction, but through a sleight of hand, your valet will have removed Dowling's money and replaced it with some worthless paper. Do you think your valet is capable of executing such a scheme?"

"Isn't a doubt. I only hired him because he's a charlatan."

"You hired him *because* he's a charlatan?"

"Needed one for my fool wife. The woman haunts me with batty notions."

"She sounds trying."

"She is trying, trying as all damnation. But she's just half my trouble. The real suffering comes from that girl of mine."

"Your daughter? You're afraid she'll be upset over the loss of the bracelet?"

"She'll raise hell about it, but that's not the worst of it. She's gotten herself engaged to some damn policeman. Already has a wife, says he's just waiting to divorce her. All the gossips in Byblos are on to it."

"You're from Byblos? Byblos, New York?" Her voice took on a slight tremor.

"All my life. But you're saying it wrong, should be *By-blows*."

So surprised was Mrs. Biddle at his revelation, she allowed the popular mispronunciation of a classical city to stand without comment, save a reflexive wince.

"Been there?" Dexter asked.

"No, I've never had that pleasure. Your daughter—is her name, by chance, Felicia?"

"Yes. That's her, Felicia."

I think, esteemed reader, we had better stop right here. There are certain details of Mrs. Biddle's life story which were left out of chapter one in the interest of brevity, but which now take on a good deal of importance.

For reasons not clear—least of all to themselves—our heroine had married a New York police detective named Biddle in early 1902. In September of that year, she insisted he give up his job and join her, at her expense, for an extended sojourn in Europe. He, being nearly as obstinate as his wife, declined to do so. Instead, he took a position in Byblos, a small city upstate. Knowing as he did his wife's thoughts on small cities upstate, his action could only be read as a challenge.

In the early part of October, Mrs. Biddle informed her husband she would be awaiting him in Étaples. He replied with directions from the New York Central depot to the room he'd rented in Byblos. Each felt sure the other would eventually give in.

Later in that same month, Mrs. Biddle learned that she was bearing his child. Had she relayed this news, he would certainly have joined her via the first available boat. But her colossal pride would not allow her to use the child to decide a contest she was certain could be won on her own terms.

Several weeks before Eugenia's birth, a school friend let her know in a letter that Biddle had become engaged to a woman named Felicia Dexter and planned to seek a divorce. It was then that Mrs. Biddle determined she would cross the Atlantic as soon as circumstances permitted. She wouldn't demean herself by fighting the divorce, but she felt she must meet this fiancée. It was beyond her conception that there could exist a woman superior to herself.

Mrs. Biddle was still recovering from the birth when the man currently calling himself Dowling contacted her about a scheme that promised, at best, a sizable payout, and at worst, a ticket to New York. That the target of this scheme was the father of her husband's bride-to-be came as something of a shock. But there seemed little chance it was anything more than coincidence.

Lord Dexter appeared not the least bit surprised that Lady Eleanor, Duchess of Aquatique, was acquainted with his daughter. "You've met the girl?"

"No. I think someone mentioned her in a letter. This policeman—not Biddle, is it?"

"Yes, that's him. You know *him*?"

"Only enough to confirm your fears," Mrs. Biddle assured him. "He is a bloodsucker of the first order."

"I knew it. Just after my money. They all are, but at least the others aren't such hypocrites."

"But your daughter cares for him?"

"Says she does. But who knows what goes through that girl's mind."

"It sounds as if you could use an ally."

Mrs. Biddle took Lord Dexter's arm in her own and led him up to the promenade deck for a stroll. By the end of their first circuit, she had amended Lady Eleanor's biography by explaining that her mother was Lydia Pashkov, boon companion to Madame Blavatsky, the *grande dame* of modern theosophy. By the end of the second circuit, his lordship was convinced of her familiarity with the occult. And by the conclusion of the third, she'd accepted a position in his entourage.

His new court theosopher then took leave of Lord Dexter to return to her cabin. It was one o'clock and her turn to tend the baby while Mélisande lunched in the dining room.

"That Polish boy, he told me he left a letter," she said. "Was there anything important in it?"

"No, only very silly. I threw it in the sea," Mélisande told her.

When she'd gone, Mrs. Biddle took out the letter the lavender-scented woman had hidden in her jewelry box. Though her German wasn't as proficient as Tomasz's, she was likewise impressed with the artist lover's frankness. A letter like this could be very useful....

7

Over the next twenty-four hours, Archie Cobb delivered no fewer than seventeen plump American lambs for the sacrificial rites conducted by Dowling at a card table in the smoking saloon. The future viscount was pleased to be sailing to this nation of braggarts. Unlike their tight-lipped British counterparts, these well-to-do Yankees couldn't help themselves from giving up their particulars to any stranger they thought worthy of impressing.

And apparently that encompassed anyone who could affect a middle-class English accent. Archie didn't have time to tell them about his fictional firm's shipping interests before they began reciting their annual income, the value of their property, and the generous allowances they gave their wife and children.

One Paterson mill owner helpfully provided both the name of his bank and the precise balance of his account, then bestowed his autograph as memento. Touched, Archie created a detailed record of their meeting and promised it would not be the last the Jersey gentleman heard from him.

Meanwhile, his new court theosopher diverted Lord Dexter with the myriad ways her occult powers could be put to use in thwarting his daughter's marriage to Biddle, the bloodsucking hypocrite and sometime policeman. So impressed was her liege lord that he set before Lady Eleanor other matters that troubled him, mostly prosaic concerns involving either his family or the municipal authorities of Byblos, and only one he thought requiring immediate attention—the crucifixion of an alderman.

Oskar, having been assured that the lost jewelry would be recovered and the thief brought to account, endeavored to occupy his mind with the comforting routine of his duties. And he was succeeding, at least until he became aware that his every movement was being followed by Tomasz, who, acting on information supplied by his adored Lady Eleanor, believed the assistant purser to be an assassin hired by her enemies.

And in cabin 176, the for-now-chastened Mélisande took up her pen. Several weeks earlier she had discovered her employer's secret journal and found its characterization of her wanting. What better use of her time than to right the matter by setting down some telling bits of her own autobiography?

It was just after luncheon on that last afternoon at sea that her mistress dispatched Mélisande to the cabin of the lavender-scented German woman with the request that she visit Lady Eleanor at her earliest convenience. Frau Kleinhempel demurred.

Yes, I know I promised not to name these characters of lesser import. But it really is rather tiresome to have to refer repeatedly to "the lavender-scented German woman." Besides, that rule was already undermined by Mélisande when the silly tart blurted the name Oskar. And since the matter *is* out of my hands, you may as well know her full name, Gertrud Kleinhempel, and that she lives with her husband in a well-appointed flat on Pilarstrasse in the posh Nymphenburg neighborhood of Munich. After all, this much could be gathered by a simple perusal of the envelope now in Mrs. Biddle's possession.

Like most of the more cosmopolitan Europeans on board the *Kronprinz Wilhelm*, the Kleinhempels were skeptical of Lady Eleanor's credentials. Though there were no public confrontations, there were numerous whispered exchanges that ended in poorly concealed titters. Frau Kleinhempel's only answer to the duchess's invitation was the Bavarian equivalent of a mocking guffaw, which sounds remarkably like the release of air brakes on a railway car. She had begun closing the door when Mélisande stopped her.

"It is about a letter of yours she has found...."

"Letter?"

"Yes, your friend, he writes very interesting letters. Good-bye, madame."

Frau Kleinhempel closed the door and sat on her bed. Thank God her husband (Christian name Luitpold, for those who are interested) was off in the smoking saloon.

Thinking her jewelry box still safe in the purser's vault, she assumed the faux duchess had gotten hold of the letter she had passed to the startled boy on that first afternoon at sea. He must be in league with this Lady Eleanor and now the faux duchess was blackmailing her. Having no money of her own, Frau Kleinhempel decided the only thing she could do was to offer a piece of her exquisite jewelry. Perhaps this so-called lady would settle for one of the lesser pendants....

The lavender-scented Frau Kleinhempel went up to the purser's office and asked for her brown leather bag. On checking the log, Oskar informed her that her husband had retrieved it the previous morning. A visibly troubled, but still lavender-scented, Frau Kleinhempel could only nod acknowledgment. The assistant purser offered a chair and she sat down, then tried to reason out what had happened.

Early in the voyage, she had become convinced her husband suspected there was something incriminating in the bag when he thrice suggested she retrieve it and display some of her costly trinkets in the dining room. Normally, he preferred that they be safely locked away. Then, beginning the day before, he made no more mention of the jewelry.

If he had retrieved the bag and seen the letter—and having as he did the emotions of a child—he would have found it impossible to keep his anger suppressed. And if he had retrieved it and *not* found the letter, why was he hiding her jewelry from her? Perhaps someone impersonating her husband had claimed the bag? She had just arrived at this thought when she saw through the porthole the startled boy to whom she had passed the *other* letter.

Tomasz had been keeping watch on the assassin Oskar when he saw the lavender-scented German lady arrive and subsequently swoon. Was no woman safe from this fiend?

Recognizing Tomasz as the inheritor of the letter with the piquant penultimate paragraph, Frau Kleinhempel rushed out to confront him.

"What have you done with my letter!" she shouted.

Reluctant to remain and discuss the matter, particularly since Frau Kleinhempel was wielding a parasol with a very sharp point like the master fencer she was, Tomasz sprinted off. The swordswoman, encumbered by her fashionably high-heeled footwear, could only shout after him. There was nothing to be done now but see what price this Lady Eleanor was demanding.

Having been one of the few titterers brave enough to titter to Lady Eleanor's face, it was with a good deal of trepidation that Frau Kleinhempel knocked on the door of the duchess's cabin.

"*Bonjour, Dame Eleanor.*"

Mrs. Biddle found her guest's French lacking. But the obsequious curtsey which accompanied it—so low it bordered on genuflection—had her complete approval.

"*Setzen Sie sich,*" she commanded, then continued in her quite adequate German. "We need not waste time. This letter has come into my possession."

She handed it to Frau Kleinhempel, who recognized it as the one she'd hidden in her jewelry box.

"You have my jewelry, too?"

"Let us say I know where it can be found."

"Are you proposing... to keep... to keep my jewelry in exchange for giving me back this letter?" Her emotions welling, the covetous Frau Kleinhempel could no longer keep back the tears.

"Dry your eyes," Mrs. Biddle told her. As a class, bourgeois housewives did not rank high in her esteem—and this frail specimen least of all. Still, she could be made use of. "You will have the return of your jewelry tonight. *Provided* you do as you're told."

"Oh, thank you, madame!"

"Your bag was dropped by a man on the boat deck yesterday morning and picked up by an associate of mine. Was it your husband who dropped it?"

"I believe it must have been, but he has said nothing."

"Then he hasn't seen the letter. I suggest you destroy it now."

Mrs. Biddle pointed to a bowl and matches on the

nearby table and Frau Kleinhempel incinerated the incendiary letter.

"When you leave here, I will send for your husband. I will tell him I have recovered the bag that he lost and will return it if he follows my instructions. He will not know you've met with me, nor will he learn of that letter. Where is he now?"

"In the smoking saloon."

"When you next see him, you shall act as if nothing has happened. Tonight, the assistant purser will come for you to identify your jewelry. Pretend to be surprised. Now, you may go."

"Forgive me, madame. But the other letter?"

"I know of no other letter."

"The boy, he was just now watching me in the purser's office. Is he not your associate?"

"No. I know nothing about him," Mrs. Biddle assured her.

II

At twenty-five minutes past three, Herr Klein-hempel made his own pilgrimage to cabin 176. A steward had handed him Mrs. Biddle's note some ten minutes earlier—just after he'd drawn the third of three kings. Her offer of information on the missing bag had not been sufficient inducement for him to abandon so promising a hand.

Though at first greatly troubled at the loss of his wife's jewelry, Herr Kleinhempel came soon to appreciate how it could be used to his advantage. He would simply deny he'd ever withdrawn the bag from the vault. Leading the authorities, he trusted, to conclude that some clever thief had impersonated him. And, most essentially, there would be no trouble with his claim on the heavily insured ornaments, because it was his own family's firm that had written the policy.

Afterward, he would explain to his wife that the lost items would, over time, be replaced. Though not stated explicitly, it would be understood that she would need to repurchase them with new proofs of affection and fidelity. The Kleinhempels were of the mercantile caste.

He greeted his hostess politely, but with none of the abject submission displayed by his wife. Mrs. Biddle was noticeably puzzled at his indifference when told she was in a position to return the jewelry.

"I will be frank, madame," he told her. "It is a matter of little importance to me whether the jewelry is recovered, or the insurance claim paid. For myself, the latter resolution offers several advantages."

"I see. So you have already written off your marriage as a loss?"

"My marriage? What would you know of that?"

"I know that few women would tolerate so obvious a scheme to defraud them of what they'd gained through... let us say, backbreaking labors. Though I suppose Frau Kleinhempel may be unique in this regard. Perhaps I was wrong to think her collection carefully chosen by one who cared deeply for such material displays of devotion. I'm sure you know best."

Herr Kleinhempel, however, was no longer sure he did know best. This ersatz aristocrat had given him second thoughts. Her characterization of his wife was uncannily accurate. But there was one last matter to be considered.

"Might I inquire if there was anything in the bag besides the jewelry and the box that held it?" he asked.

"What is it you have in mind?"

"Oh, a letter perhaps?"

"No, there were no letters, no paper of any sort."

"And you searched it thoroughly?"

"Need I answer that, Herr Kleinhempel?"

"No, that will not be necessary. Tell me, madame, what is it you want in return for the bag?"

"Only your cooperation in catching the thief."

"You are unusually generous, madame. Might I ask why?"

"I wish this man to get what he deserves, but under circumstances of my choosing."

"So he is the man who recovered my bag?"

"Is that important?" she asked curtly.

"I think it would be to him."

"He will be getting no more than his due. These are my terms—you may accept them or not."

"I accept, madame. But only on your assurance I will not be accusing an innocent man."

"You will not need to make any accusation. Tonight, the assistant purser will come to your cabin. It might be quite late. He will tell you he has found the man who has your jewels. All you need do is identify them."

"Very well, madame."

Herr Kleinhempel made a short bow and left intending to return to his card game. But on the promenade deck, his fetching wife surprised him. She took him by the arm.

"Oh, Luitpold. Where have you been? You spend all your time away."

This time, the lavender-scented lady's irresistible look did not fail her. There was a great release of tension in the Kleinhempels' cabin that afternoon, and, after a light supper, it continued well into the evening.

At ten o'clock, Mrs. Biddle located Oskar in the purser's office and asked for his master key.

"My key, madame?"

"Do you, or do you not, want to recover the jewelry?" Oskar surrendered his key and she resumed. "At midnight, go to my cabin and the girl will give you instructions. Bring along two stewards. Understood?"

"Yes, madame."

When she emerged, Tomasz came up beside her.

"Lady Eleanor, what are you doing speaking with that assassin? You should be more careful."

"Setting a trap," she told him. "And I need your help."

"Anything at all."

"Come to my cabin at 11:30. The girl will tell you just what needs to be done."

"I will be there, madame."

Mrs. Biddle then went to the cabin of the man currently calling himself Dowling.

"It's all arranged," he told her. "Archie will have Dexter in the reading room at midnight. Do you have the key?"

She handed him Oskar's key.

"Afterwards, you and Archie and I will reassemble here to divide the winnings."

"Tonight?" she asked. "I'd think tomorrow would be soon enough."

"Yes, no doubt you would. But I think Archie and I will sleep easier if it's taken care of tonight."

"All right. I understand you've been doing well for yourself at the table."

"Yes, and I don't mind telling you now that it was

essential that I did so. That damn Céleste cleaned me out." The tired old man looked at her as if asking for sympathy, and for a brief moment, his daughter almost allowed him some. But then he added, "Women have always been my Achilles' heel."

Mrs. Biddle shook her head in disgust and left him.

III

The reading room of the *Kronprinz Wilhelm* closed at exactly eleven o'clock each night. At 10:45, Mrs. Biddle entered the room carrying a brown leather bag. She placed it on the floor and sat down to read a magazine. Then, using her foot, she silently edged the bag under the skirting of a table. When the attendant rang his bell, she left for the Vienna Café and a prearranged meeting with Archie Cobb.

"When you go in, set yourself up at the table at the bow end," she told him. "The bag is already in place."

"All right. Do you think your father suspects?"

"Not that I can tell. How much did he raise?"

"Must be at least five thousand, but I only know from hearsay. Dexter has me a little worried. Never met a man so difficult to get a bead on."

"He's not so different from the typical self-made American yokel. They make a religion of individualism, but it usually amounts to little more than enshrined eccentricities."

"Enshrined eccentricities is right—man's as queer as Dick's hatband."

Mrs. Biddle was not familiar with Dick, or his pro-verbial hatband, but she seldom felt Archie's aphorisms worthy of exploration.

"Another cognac," she called to the waiter.

At exactly 11:30, Tomasz arrived at cabin 176.

"You cut your face," Mélisande said to him.

Touching his cheek, Tomasz only now realized that Frau Kleinhempel's parasol had drawn blood. He let the girl dab at it with a moistened handkerchief.

"It was necessary," he lied, "to protect Lady Eleanor. Is she here?"

"No, she comes later. She tells me to get you ready."

She'd removed his jacket before he could object. But when she began loosening his tie, he jumped back.

"You must stop this! I have come to help Lady Eleanor."

"Yes, yes. I know. But you see, Lady Eleanor is very lonely...."

"Has she read my letter?"

"Yes, three times she read it. It makes her very... hot."

"Hot?"

"Yes, she goes for a walk to cool down...."

"Then I should go to her."

"No, she wants you to stay here. You see, she likes you very much, but..."

"But what?"

"Well...." Mélisande brought her face to his shoulder and sniffed. "She says, she thinks maybe you need a bath."

It was true that with one thing and another Tomasz had let matters of hygiene slip from his mind. In fact, he hadn't bathed since he left his Chelsea boarding house. And for two days he'd been wearing the same clothes.

"I will see if the steward can arrange for me to use one of the baths."

"No, no. Why do that? We have a bath here."

"But..."

For ten minutes, his outsized modesty held his ardor at bay. But when Oskar arrived at midnight, Tomasz could be heard splashing lustily and singing a Polish love song.

Mélisande entered the bathroom and began picking up his clothes.

"What are you doing?" he asked.

"I will have them washed for you."

"At this time of night?"

"Yes, the laundryman is my friend. You wait here. If the baby cries, you give her the bottle. Good-bye."

"But..."

Mélisande closed the door and hid his clothes under the bed. Then she went with Oskar to fetch a thoroughly relaxed Herr Kleinhempel and his gainfully talented wife.

In the meantime, Dowling, Dexter, Mrs. Biddle, and Archie had assembled in the reading room. Both Dexter's carpetbag and Dowling's brown leather case were handed to Archie and he took them to the table nearest the bow. There he pretended to count the contents, carefully removing and replacing the same stacks of real currency repeatedly. He announced both totaled more than $100,000, with Dexter having a $3,000 advantage.

The bidding moved quickly to $90,000. But then Lord Dexter paused. He asked to see the deed again and inspected it carefully. The left eyebrow looked keen enough, but the right was unmoved. His lordship took them into private conference by approaching a window and staring out into the night.

Meanwhile, the others fidgeted in their seats. Dowling was nervous that he'd taken the bidding too high. Archie was nervous that Dowling had noticed him replacing his brown leather bag with the one that held Frau Kleinhempel's jewelry. Mrs. Biddle's fidgeting was not, of course, due to nerves, but merely to the fact she'd left the Vienna Café after three cognacs without visiting the Ladies' Toilette.

Once he was convinced he had all three squirming, Lord Dexter returned and secured the deed by making his unbeatable maximum bid.

Dowling shrugged and offered Dexter his hand.

"Well, fair is fair, I suppose. No one can say I didn't give it my best. I will inform the syndicate that they will now need to contact you."

He picked up the brown leather bag from the table and was halfway to the door when Oskar entered, accompanied by two stewards.

"Excuse me, sir. But that bag—it has been reported stolen."

"Nonsense. I had it in the vault until this afternoon."

"Then you won't mind if we examine it?"

"I do mind."

"Forgive me, sir," Oskar told him, "but finding you in a room closed at this hour, I'm afraid I must insist." He then motioned to one of the stewards, who went to the corridor and returned with the Kleinhempels.

"Is this your bag?" he asked Herr Kleinhempel.

"It looks like it, yes."

Oskar placed it on a table and opened it, then removed the oblong jewelry box. The lavender-scented lady rushed forward and assured herself her collection was intact.

"My bag must have gotten switched with theirs," Dowling protested.

Instead of responding, Oskar removed a small bundle from the bag and unwrapped it.

"My damn daughter's bracelet!" Lord Dexter exclaimed. His eyebrows, still somewhat puzzled by the course of events, quietly signaled their satisfaction via a stately allemande.

"If it was a simple mix-up of bags, how is it that this gentleman's bracelet found its way into it as well?" Oskar asked Dowling.

Dowling looked up at the only one present capable of engineering such treachery.

"You, my dear?"

"I've no idea what you're talking about."

While Oskar had the stewards lead the culprit to his cabin with orders that he be kept under watch, Frau Kleinhempel examined the bracelet he'd just uncovered.

"Oh, Luitpold. Isn't it the most beautiful thing you've ever seen?"

Herr Kleinhempel had heard those words many times before and the outcome was nearly always the same. So it would be again. He was, after all, still feeling contrite for having wrongly suspected his wife. And certainly the affection she'd lavished that afternoon was deserving of some form of... commemoration.

Archie and Mrs. Biddle both left the room $2,700 the richer. But it was Timothy Dexter who came out on top. Herr Kleinhempel's check for $8,000 amounted to a 60% return on the bracelet. What's more, he succeeded in pocketing what he dubbed the "comely deed" without spending a dollar of Confederate currency.

8

On her way out of the reading room, Mrs. Biddle came upon Mélisande observing the scene from the shadows.

"The baby!" she reminded the girl.

"It's OK. Your lover is there, he waits for you."

Back in their cabin, they found Tomasz dressed in a flowery kimono with Eugenia in his lap, humming a lullaby.

"Lady Eleanor, at last..."

"M. Szczęsny, I'm sorry. I was detained. And now it's so very late. But I expect we will be seeing a good deal of one another. Lord Dexter has offered me a position in his court."

"A position in his court?"

"Yes, I'm to be his theosopher."

"You're coming to Byblos?"

"Yes, I am."

"That is wonderful!"

"Well, we shall see about that. But perhaps now we should all get some sleep?"

"Yes, yes, of course."

Mélisande reached under the bed and brought out his clothing in a heap. Tomasz took it up and made a short bow. Then, as he toddled happily off to his cabin, Mrs. Biddle dashed for the bathroom—the three cognacs had waited long enough.

The next morning, Mélisande asked about this "By-blos."

"It's a few hours from New York. I've never been there, but don't expect much."

"Why don't we stay in New York?" the girl asked.

"Because there is something I must see to in Byblos. If you come and help me, I will give you enough to come back to New York later."

"How long?"

"A month, maybe more, maybe less."

"How much will you give me?"

"Five hundred dollars. Agreed?"

"OK. But I will see a little of New York before we go to... Byblos?"

"Yes, but we will be taking a morning train tomorrow. There's one more thing. We must travel separately. I can't be seen with the baby. When we get to Byblos, you and she will stay elsewhere. I'll come whenever I can. Now I have something to give you." She removed a fifty-dollar bill from her bag and held it out to Mélisande. The girl grabbed it, but Mrs. Biddle had not yet released her end. "It's not a gift. You are to use this only in an emergency."

"Emergency?"

"*Dans les circonstances critiques.*" Only when the girl nodded did Mrs. Biddle release her end of the banknote. "The most important thing to remember is that you can trust no one, including my associates."

"Associates?"

"The people I'm traveling with, Cobb and Dexter."

"What about the Polish boy?"

"What about him? You haven't gone soft on him, have you?"

"Bah! No, I have not gone soft on him. But he does not seem dangerous."

"Well, he may be a danger of a different sort. Don't tell him you're going to Byblos."

"I'll tell him I'm going home to Pittsbourg."

"Yes, tell him you're going home to Pittsbourg," Mrs. Biddle smiled.

It was almost noon when the *Kronprinz Wilhelm* finally docked at the Lloyd line's Hoboken pier. Lord Dexter and his party were at the front of the queue, but this time the aristocrats were forced to give way. First off the boat would be the two New York police detectives who'd boarded with the pilot off Sandy Hook. Accompanying them was the man sometimes known as Dowling—though five weeks before, when taken into custody by the same two detectives, he had been using the name Leyland. As he passed his daughter, he stopped and addressed her, sotto voce.

"You may consider your share a christening gift for my granddaughter. But you may be sure," he went on, turning now to encompass Archie Cobb, "both of you may be sure, I'll be looking you up in your new home."

Mrs. Biddle looked over him to the policemen. "Please take that tiresome old man away." Then she looked over her shoulder at Cobb.

"I never said a word about the child," Archie quickly assured her.

The tension was broken when a grateful Oskar came forward and offered to escort Lady Eleanor off the boat. To Tomasz, still laboring under the misapprehension that the assistant purser was a hired assassin, his approach bore all the hallmarks of an assault. The misguided Pole flung himself at Oskar, but with such a complete lack of precision that he soon found himself sailing over the rail of the gangplank. As his jacket billowed in the wind, a well-thumbed page of writing paper slipped from an inside pocket and was sent skyward by a sudden updraft. Unhappily, the gust did nothing to delay Tomasz's rendezvous with the malodorous brine below.

Once he'd fished out his secretary and lied his way through Customs, Lord Dexter took his ill-equipped entourage on a shopping spree. Archie would need a wardrobe befitting the Viscount of Abernethy, Lady Eleanor the garb of a theosopher—and Tomasz something that didn't smell of Hoboken bilge water. But the first order of business was to replace the bracelet for his daughter that he'd sold to Herr Kleinhempel.

Mrs. Biddle suggested a visit to Tiffany's, and there helped him choose a replacement which compensated for its comparative lack of craftsmanship with more, and larger, diamonds. At $6,000 it came dearer than the original, but with the profit from the latter's sale and the avoidance of duty, Lord Dexter calculated that he was still ahead $3,200.

Herr Kleinhempel wasn't so lucky avoiding the duty that afternoon, there being a discrepancy between the customs form he'd carefully filled out the evening before and the contents of his wife's jewelry box. They'd spent a trying hour extricating themselves and were only now arriving at their Manhattan hotel.

While her husband paid the driver, Frau Kleinhempel descended from the cab with the help of the doorman. Just as she reached the sidewalk, a page of stationery carried by a strong breeze wafted against her face. It bore a familiar scent. She took it in her hand and read.... Mein Gott! It was the compromising letter with the piquant penultimate paragraph!

The next moment, her husband was coming toward her. "What's that, my dear?"

In one deft movement, the lavender-scented lady crumpled the page into her fist and swooned. The doorman caught her and brought her to a bench.

"Quick," he told Herr Kleinhempel, "go inside and fetch a doctor."

As soon as her husband was safely away, Frau Kleinhempel opened a wary eye and began eating the piquant letter. The doorman, of course, noticed nothing, and for three weeks he and his wife dined off of his discretion.

Meanwhile, Tomasz, still damp from his dunking and bearing a scent quite unlike lavender, had been sent to settle with Tiffany's cashier while the others of his party retired to a cozy café just down the street. He counted out sixty of the apricot-toned banknotes Lord Dexter had given him and then waited for the cashier to hand him the receipt. Later that afternoon, after satisfying Tiffany & Co. with a check drawn on a New York bank, his playful employer bailed him out at the Jefferson Market Police Court.

Lady Eleanor begged off dinner that evening. She was exhausted, she told the others, and would have something brought to her. At seven o'clock, she left her room on the fifth floor of the Plaza Hotel and stole down to that of Mélisande one floor below. She came bearing gifts.

"Where have you been?" the girl asked. "I haven't seen any of New York."

"You've plenty of time. I've brought you some things."

Mrs. Biddle set the packages on the bed and one by

one Mélisande opened them and donned their contents. When she had finished, she looked the part of a sophisticated American girl, though undoubtedly one of moderate means. Mrs. Biddle's generosity only went so far.

"Go down to the lobby," she instructed while adding a silver brooch to the ensemble. "A Miss Springer will meet you there. Miriam Springer. I told her you are the daughter of a French artist."

"Who is Miss Springer?"

"A friend of mine. She will show you New York." Mrs. Biddle took out another fifty dollars and handed it to Mélisande.

"Is this from my five hundred dollars?" the girl asked.

"No. This is for tonight."

"How could I spend fifty dollars in one night?"

"You've never been to New York. Remember, don't let Miss Springer out of your sight. And *do not* take up with any men. They aren't all like those boys you met in Étaples. Now go, and be back by dawn. We catch an early train."

Mélisande gave her a peck on the cheek and went off. She was very pleased, and sincerely grateful. But as she waited for the elevator, she took off the simple silver brooch and replaced it with the colorful cloisonné one the lady in cabin 12 had provided her.

That night, and for many more to follow, Eugenia slumbered to the drip... drip... drip... of American plumbing.

Thus ends the first novella in the Byblos Foretold series. I do so hope you've enjoyed it, and that it's whetted your appetite for the second course of this sumptuous verbal feast. You see, it just so happens that the second novella, *Peddlers All*, is on sale and awaiting your pleasure. In it, you will find my gripping account of how I come to be telling this most extraordinary saga.

Those curious as to how Mélisande spent her evening in New York may wish to read "An Outing on Manhattan," the second tale in Mélisande's own book, *The Fly Maiden's Book of Virtues*, which is available to the most devoted of readers.

Both can be found at the **ByblosForetold.com** web site.

Glossary

cold deck : a crooked deck of cards

expectorial : involving spittle

fly : street-wise; hip

gadoue : French slang for a low prostitute

genetrix : a woman who has given birth

queer : counterfeit

Byblos Foretold: The Great Novaplex

What is a novaplex? Put simply, it is a revolutionary literary form which transcends the limits of the novel and challenges the conventions of the marketplace. More specifically, Byblos Foretold is the complex chronicle of an extraordinary troupe of Americans—native and émigré, rich and poor, ruthless and artful, and even, occasionally, sympathetic.

But most of all, this is a work in progress. If you would like to follow developments, you need only stop by **ByblosForetold.com**

– M.E. Meegs